About the Author

I have always had a passion for setting myself goals in life, something to strive for, something to achieve against all the odds, most of my life has been against the odds.

I love problem solving and enjoy helping anyone who may need my help.

I have a great love and passion for creating food from around the world, I believe that could have been another path in life for me to be a chef and own a restaurant.

My love of history still remains with me today, and buildings, very old buildings still hold such an interest to me.

I live in a very old Victorian house built in 1837, the moment I entered the building I fell in love with it and knew straight away this is my home, I feel honoured and very lucky as it is a listed building, it's very cold in the winter months but a small price to pay for the privilege to once again be part of history.

Dedication

This book is dedicated to my mother Nancy Critcher, thank you for your love and strength and for always teaching us to fight for your rights and beliefs and to always have faith in your own abilities against the greatest odds.
Never to be bitter, always find a way to forgive, but never forget and to always remain a free spirit in mind, body and soul.

My dearest sister, Paula Lawson Philips, thank you for your love and support, love you forever, Big Sis.

Clare Lee, my friend of 30 years, yesterday is history, tomorrow is a mystery.

Ivan Critcher my brother, what can I say, you have been the best brother I am lucky enough to have, no matter what, if I need you I know you will always be there, love you lots.

My son Ross, I thank you from the bottom of my heart for never letting me down and always being there to pick me up when I have fallen down, I was once your purple soft satin pillow to safely land on in your dark days.
Thank you for giving me a purple soft satin pillow to land on when I myself have needed it, I love you with all my heart.

My angel sister Hazel, missing you so much, I know you are looking down on me and that fills my heart with a warm glow.

My ray of sunshine full of love colour, and so much laughter my granddaughter Scarlett Mai Johnstone, (Pickle) you keep my days so bright and fill my heart with happiness each and every day, Nanny loves you.

Esther Lawson

WOGAMATTER

AUSTIN MACAULEY
PUBLISHERS LTD.

A CIP catalogue record for this title is available from the British Library.

ISBN 9781784552909 (Paperback)
ISBN 9781786294036 (Hardback)
ISBN 9781786294043 (E-Book)

www.austinmacauley.com

First Published (2016)
Austin Macauley Publishers Ltd.
25 Canada Square
Canary Wharf
London
E14 5LQ

Acknowledgements

I would like to acknowledge my son, Ross Johnstone, for his fabulous illustrated artwork for the cover of my book *Wogamatter*.

I would also like to acknowledge West Sussex Social Services for all their invaluable positive help in looking after me and my family when we needed it most.

I would like to acknowledge Austin Macauley Publishers for giving me the chance to publish my book and for all their support throughout the process.

I also acknowledge the full support of my mother, Nancy Critcher, it has been difficult for you to go back into the past to give me clarification on certain points of information.

Thank you Clare Lee, my friend of 30 years, I acknowledge all your support through every step of writing this book.

Chapter 1

I was born on the 12th May 1962 in the Borough of Camberwell, South East London.

The day I was born my destiny was already written out for me (born to fight).

My registered birth name was Valerie Mary Lawson.

My parents' names were Nancy Ensi Lawson (formerly Paulis), Mother, and Joseph Leslie Lawson (Parachute Instructor), Father.

My mother was born in Kenya, East Africa to parents of French and Sri Lankan descent.

Kenya was a British Colony, and my mum was born a British Subject with a legal right to enter the United Kingdom.

My father was in the British Army (Red Signals) and was over in Kenya fighting in the Mau Mau war, that is how he met my mother; it was not long before they got married because my mum got pregnant.

My mother was only 16 years old when my father brought her over to England to give birth to me, and then to be abandoned in London in the 1960s, a country in which racism was rife and the hostility towards blacks was insurmountable and to top it all, Mum did not speak fluent English; the only languages my mother spoke very well were French and Swahili, so you can imagine the absolute distress this caused her, totally terrified and in a very hostile and aggressive country at the time.

12, Dagmar Road, Camberwell South East London was my home address, but not for long.

The building was a very old Edwardian building and in previous times I would imagine that it held the finer people of life, with the lower downstairs basement probably the servants' quarters.

The house was converted into flats and we lived in the very top flat, my grandmother Cath, my father's mother lived in the flats below us.

It wasn't very long before word got out that a black woman was living in their street and this was not to be tolerated by the local residents living in Dagmar road; they wanted my mother out, myself included.

Mum kept herself to herself and always paid her rent on time and kept a very clean flat, but that didn't make any difference, we were black and had to go.

One day the landlord who owned the property knocked on my mother's door and said to her,

"I am so sorry Mrs Lawson, I have to give you notice to vacate this dwelling with immediate effect as soon as possible, it's not what I want to do but my hands are tied, it's all the residents that want you out and I have been put in an intolerable situation, you understand don't you."

My mother went to the downstairs flat to speak to my grandmother about what the landlord had just told her, "Cath, the man who collects the rent has just told me that I have to get out and go and live somewhere else, I just don't know what to do, I don't know where Lou is, I haven't seen him in ages."

Lou was a nickname that everyone used instead of Joseph; my father hated the name Joseph and would never have himself addressed by that name.

"Yes, I already know all about it Nancy, the landlord came and spoke to me telling me he had no choice, but as for Lou, he is in prison love, and is due out tomorrow."

"Prison... prison, why is he in prison? How come you didn't tell me this before, I was left all on my own to go into hospital and have my baby, and you couldn't even be bothered to tell me what was going on, no, no I want to go back home to Kenya and I am taking Val with me."

"Come on Nancy, don't be like that, Lou told me not to tell you anything, Lou will be out tomorrow, we can both talk to him then."

That was my welcome into the world.

My father was back and met me for the first time two months after I was born and that is when I was finally registered that I existed and had been born.

My grandmother had told my father that he better get himself back into the Army as quickly as possible as my mother had been told that she has to get out of the flat, no blacks in this street. My father re-entered the army and was given temporary accommodation at a wimpy hotel in London.

Shortly afterwards news arrived, my father and his family had to report to Emsworth Army barracks in Hampshire.

In April 1963 my sister was born, my mum had a very difficult pregnancy and was very ill suffering with severe anemia and was very underweight, the doctor was very worried about her physical state of health and said that she had not given herself a chance for her body to make a full recovery after giving birth to me 11 months before.

Shortly after my sister was born, my father dragged my mother into the bedroom and threw her on the bed and proceeded to smack her about and started strangling her whilst he was raping her. I was in my cot and started crying and screaming and with that my father got up and left the room, my mother was still very sore and had not healed properly from the birth of my sister.

Heavily pregnant with my next sister Hazel, she was visited again by the Army doctor who was gravely concerned with her health; she was very underweight, nearly skin and bone, and had deteriorated even further and at great risk to her carrying another child with barely any chance of her body having time to recover after the two previous pregnancies.

The doctor said to my mum, "You really have to start eating some more and gain weight, if you don't do this, then I have to warn you that your life is at risk, you will not be strong enough or well enough to go full term with this pregnancy, have you not heard of birth control? Ok Mrs Lawson I will come and see you next week, it's important that I keep a very close eye on you."

My mother was getting very close to her term ready to give birth to my sister Hazel only a few weeks to go, when suddenly there was a knock at the door; some army officials and they needed to talk to her urgently, "Mrs Lawson, we are sorry to inform you, we have had orders to take your Army allowance book away from you, your husband Private Lawson is out of it, no longer in the Army."

Mum said, "What do you mean, out of it? How can I manage with my children if you are taking my book away from me, where is my husband?"

"All we can tell you Mrs Lawson is that he is now in prison, and that's all the information we can give you at this moment in time, you will have to leave the Army married quarters, but we have taken your condition into consideration, your health issues and also the other smaller children, and we have arranged for the Army welfare to come and speak to you later on today. Try not to worry Mrs Lawson, we are not going to throw you out onto the streets, we are very sympathetic to the situation you have been placed in."

"We are also aware that you have drawn your allowance yesterday, and have decided that you may keep that payment, but if you don't mind I am so sorry, can we have the allowance book?"

She handed the book over, absolutely devastated and worried out of her mind, in shock about what had just been told to her. She kept all feelings and emotions locked inside, she was not the sort of person to allow anyone to see her personal feelings then she said, "Thank you, where am I going to find somewhere to live, I don't know how to find another home."

"As I have said before Mrs Lawson, don't worry we will help you, the Army welfare is coming to see you today and they will sort everything out."

The Army sorted everything out for us; they had even sorted the National Assistance as it was then known in the 1960s, DHSS, so at least she had some form of money coming in to help support herself and us children.

The Army was kind enough to take us to our new accommodation via army transportation from Emsworth, Hampshire to Angmering, West Sussex.

We had nothing, only our personal possessions and clothes, nothing much at all. We moved into a pre-fabricated 2-bedroom bungalow which had been specially erected to accommodate homeless families.

When we arrived there was nothing whatsoever except a mattress which we all had to share and sleep on; Mum, my two sisters and me, I was 3 years old and remember this well, but I couldn't really understand why I didn't have my own bed.

Slowly but surely our home was becoming a home, I remember distinctly getting very excited that a bed was coming and no longer did we have to sleep on a mattress on the floor.

Mr and Mrs Jones were the caretakers of the Bungalows, any problems that occurred or even if you needed to buy secondhand furniture, they were the people you spoke to.

They had their own property outside the confines of the bungalows made especially for homeless families, and the dividing line to accentuate this was a wall encasing us and a big white gate. I remember as a child standing many times just looking through this white gate and watching the world go by, unaware of the situation and totally unembarrassed that we were considered the dregs of society, the bottom of the barrel.

It was a beautiful warm sunny day and I had my most favourite dress on, it was a very lightweight cotton dress, white in colour with big orange spots. I felt free in it and enjoyed feeling the warm summer rays pouring onto my skin. On this glorious day, Mum held me by the hand and was taking me through the white gate, to the left hand side of me was Mr and Mrs Jones's bungalow and to the right hand side of me was a very large flint stone building with a green barn size door. I could see Mr Jones opening up the door and we were heading in his direction.

"Good Morning Mrs Lawson, how are you today, you are very lucky as I have had some more bits and pieces delivered yesterday, I think they will be suitable for what you are looking for."

Mum was very shy of people and just managed to quietly say hello back.

I myself was very excited and couldn't wait to get inside and see what this was all about. Mr Jones opened the door halfway and proceeded inside, my mother following behind him and then me; it was quite dark and I couldn't really see properly what was inside until Mr Jones decided it was better to open up the doors fully to reveal the hidden treasure.

What I saw in my little mind at the time was delightful; there were wardrobes, coffee tables, beds, clothes, pots and pans kitchen tables, flower printed glasses in lemon and orange, knives and forks, toys teddies, it really was an Aladdin's cave.

I heard Mr Jones say to Mum that she could only pick 3 items at any one time and would have to pay in weekly installments until it was all fully paid up, then she was allowed to come again and pick 3 more items and start the process all over again.

Mum took her time choosing her 3 items very carefully, making sure that every item chosen was a priority. There tucked away in the corner was a beautiful Victorian chaise longue and Mum chose to have that as we didn't have anything to sit on at home. I was getting bored very quickly and was starting to feel very cold being inside this old flint stone building and was showing signs of wanting to go. I saw Mum hand over some money to Mr Jones and in return he gave her this little brown payments booklet and said that he would try his hardest to get the items over to her later on this evening as he knew how desperate she was.

I remember many times going to this building with Mum, the sight, smell and feeling of this building remained with me for the rest of my life.

During this process, Mum was building up our home and at this stage, I have no recollection of my father being present; the memories I do have are fond memories of just us and Mum. I remember her making up a little picnic and being very excited that she was taking us out on the beach which was just a 10-minute walk away. She would take us for little walks in the countryside to see the horses and give an apple or two, she was a great mum who had so little yet gave us so much and showered us with so much love, I can still remember those feelings now and it fills me with a warm happy, safe glow; if it was edible I would eat it over and over again.

As a little family we were settled as best we could be, Mum got us into our little routines and we were happy, however those happy times did not last for long and future events that were just about to happen would change our lives forever.

It was early evening, my sisters were in bed and me being me wanted to stay up with Mum, to sit with her quietly watching the lovely glow and listening to the crackles and popping of the coal fire; for some reason I found it very soothing, it created a feeling of being safe. Mum was in her nightdress and doing her hair and in the 1960s curlers was the nightly regime, preparing herself for bedtime, when suddenly there was a loud knocking at the backdoor and I heard a man's voice saying, "Nancy, Nancy open the door let me in, it's Lou."

I remember my mum muttering to herself as she was getting up to go and open the door, "What the hell does he want?"

I was sitting at the bottom end of the chaise longue and didn't move an inch and carried on playing with my toy.

Mum came back into the lounge and resumed her position and carried on putting her curlers in, and I saw this man rip through with some bags in his hands and disappear into the hallway where the bathroom and bedrooms are. I could smell straightaway a very strong smell that filled the lounge like some thick fog, I didn't know at the time what this smell was but later on in my life I got to know and recognise this smell as the putrid smell of alcohol and my association with this smell was fear and sheer terror.

The man that I had seen rip through our lounge was in fact my father and when he came back into the lounge, I looked at him and looked at him again and had some recollection that I knew this face. The first words my father managed to splutter out were, "What's she doing sitting there?" in a thick Liverpool accent.

My little heart started pounding and I was beginning to feel very afraid and felt that something not nice was about to happen. I looked at Mum with the movement of my eyes only, and I could see she was not herself, her hands were shaking and she kept dropping her comb and curlers. The next thing that happened as he walked slowly towards the fireplace he snapped through gritted teeth, "Nancy you've been sleeping with other men haven't you, think I don't know, I've had my friends keeping an eye on you."

Mum then said in a timid voice, "Your friends are telling you a load of rubbish, I've been here with my children building up a home, I wouldn't do anything like that, I am too afraid of people, you are drunk and just want to search for an argument Lou."

With a quick snap, he lunged forwards to where Mum was sitting, within seconds my father had her nearly off the floor by her hair. I was so terrified and ran over near to the fireplace, watching, hearing Mum crying and whimpering, "No, get off me Lou, get off me."

I was standing there not knowing what to do, my father then started throwing her on the chaise longue like some lifeless rag doll, then the punches were coming full throttle, one, two, three; his movements repeating over and over again. Mum's arms going up and down in every which way she could to try and deflect the punches, in order to get some kind protection from the ferocious blows that were descending upon her tiny thin frame of a body.

The next thing, my father had hold of Mum's head in his hands, the same way you would hold a ball, then he smashed her head on the arm rest of the chaise longue, I heard an almighty crack and noticed straightaway that the arm rest had completely broken, no longer in its glorified upright position, just flopping downwards, destroyed and no longer an object of beauty.

I was so frightened, I must have gone into some kind of shock, I looked down to the floor and saw my doll at my feet, I was standing in a puddle, it was urine. I had peed myself and was so scared that I was going to be in trouble for wetting myself, but the next thing I knew, Mum had grabbed me and taken me to her bedroom and closed the door.

Mum carried on crying and was looking at the damage she had received at the hands of my father; she had bruises to her face, a lopsided fat lip, and when she lifted her nightdress I could see straightaway bruises to the left hand side of her ribs; looking back into my mind's eye she was so painfully skinny, it was like stretched skin over bone.

After she had cleaned herself up and made herself as comfortable as her body would allow, she got into bed and started crying again, softly whimpering and saying to me that she didn't want him in her life, "Oh Val what am I going to do."

I said to Mum, "Mummy, I don't like him, he hurts you, I will protect you Mummy, I will."

The promise I made that night remains in place up to this present day. I cuddled up to her feeling safe and went to sleep.

I awoke to the gentle tugging of my arm, it was Mum saying in a whisper, "Val, Val wake up, I have made Hazel's bottle and I want you to go and give it to her, I want you to stay in the bedroom with your sisters, I will come and tell you when it's time for breakfast."

Of course me being me wanted to investigate where my father had got to, so instead of going into the bedroom where my sisters were, I decided that I would have a quick look in the lounge area. I gently pushed the door open just enough to allow myself a view inside the room and there I saw my father fast asleep on the now broken chaise longue and with that my sister Hazel started crying and wanting her bottle.

Hazel was standing up in her cot crying and wanting her bottle, she was also soaking wet. I knew I had to go and tell my mum that she needed her nappy seeing to, and my other sister was awake, I told her to stay where she was and I was going to go and get Mummy.

As I came into the lounge my father was no longer spilled out over the chaise longue, I could hear my father talking to my mum saying that he was sorry and that he swears on the lives of the kids he will never do it again, I could hear him saying, "Come on Nancy, I love you and the kids so much, I want my family back, I promise I will get a job and no more prison, give me another chance, you will see I really mean it."

I never heard Mum utter one word, I went through into the kitchen and duly told my mum that Hazel needed seeing to, after that I ran as fast as I could straight back into my bedroom.

The house during the day stayed very subdued, we were quietly playing in our bedroom, but again, me being me wasn't happy about being stuck in the bedroom, it was not the normal thing, we always played wherever Mum was, so I gathered my sisters and told them to follow me.

When we all arrived in the lounge we could see that Mum was not in the lounge and could hear her talking with our father in the kitchen. When we entered the kitchen I could smell an awful smell with a blue smoke haze, it was the stinking smell of tobacco. My father got up and scooped Hazel into his arms, me and my other sister ran straight over to our mum, clutching onto her legs, our father put Hazel back down and she came to join us.

When Mum moved we moved with her like three little ducklings bobbing up and down, any ripple in the water taking us away from our mother and we would quickly re-paddle, three little ducklings on the pond feeling unsafe when the chain got broken, how she never fell over is beyond me.

Life now was with our mother and father and soon things were becoming harmonious, a calming lull descending upon us. My father had kept his word, no alcohol and no more beating Mum up, we had become a happy little full family unit.

I had soon forgotten about the brutal attacks I had witnessed perpetrated against my mother by my father. It was nice playing games with Dad and my sisters; we were now beginning to trust him. My father built a little wild bird sanctuary and would put injured birds in there, fix broken wings, all sorts of things then set them free back into the wild to get on with their own little lives saved by the hands of my father. I used to get so much joy standing alongside him, watching all the loving repairs he would do on the birds and occasionally he would allow me to give the birds a stroke or two.

I was now enjoying all the happy things that were present in our lives, my dad back in the family unit, and a big surprise my father's mother, my grandmother, coming to visit and stay for a few weeks. I thought she was lovely with all the gifts and presents she brought along with her for us children, especially the sweets, we were in heaven. A particular present I enjoyed so much was a blackboard with chalk, my sisters couldn't wait to get their hands on it much to my disapproval then a quick click of the camera and that momentous occasion captured forever.

Today I look back at the old black and white photograph and remember how lovely that day was with my sisters and grandmother.

It was getting close to the time for my grandmother to leave and return to London where she lived and the day just before she was due to leave, it was decided that she was taking us to the beach for the day. We were all so excited – a day at the beach with our Nan, I remember this day so very well, the sights and the smell of the sea, the complete fun and laughter running in and out of the water, Nan chasing us laughing and then helping us make sandcastles with our buckets and spades and sitting down to well-deserved orange ice lollipops. I managed to accidently get sand on mine and every time I tried to lick it I would have a gritty sensation in my mouth, so decided to push my ice-lolly into the sand and leave it there; to this day I can't eat orange ice lollipops because of the memory of the gritty sand in my mouth.

There is an old black and white photograph of me on the beach in my little bikini with my grandmother behind me, this was the very last time any photograph would ever be taken with our grandmother.

My father was working as a chef at some restaurant, wages were coming into the family household on a regular basis and life was good, until one Friday being payday, there were no signs of my father returning home from work. This of course caused my mum great worry as she had no money and was waiting for my father's return so she could go and do the weekly shopping – she had just about run out of everything. I remember being given a bowl of cornflakes for tea, I thought this was odd but still enjoyed having the cornflakes anyway.

Saturday morning, then afternoon, still no sign of my father. By this time I was feeling very hungry, no breakfast or lunch, the pressure was on, what an earth was she going to do, three young children and pregnant again and this time with twins.

I had let Mum know how hungry we were and she was just preparing something for us to eat; Mum had found a bag of flour and was busy making some bread rolls which to me was taking a very long time. I could smell the bread cooking in the oven and this was making me feel worse, I had never experienced such pain in my stomach, the only way I can explain what I felt was like knives repeatedly jabbing inside your stomach lasting for a few moments and becoming more and more intense as time went by, and the only way to find some relief from this pain was to cry, and the more I cried the better I felt. Little did I know that I was to have these pains throughout my childhood.

Sunday morning my father had returned with a bag of dead chickens with their heads still on and with all the feathers, he told my mum that he couldn't help it and how sorry he was. His mates asked him to come to the pub for a quick pint at lunch time after they had finished their shift, this led on to drinking for the rest of the day going into the night and he had spent the night at his mates' house. Come Saturday they all went to the bookies to gamble on horse racing then went onto the pub again and stayed another night at his mates' house, all the wages completely gone, blown on his self-indulgence, not taking into consideration his wife and young family, only to return with a bag full of dead chickens.

My mother gave him one more chance to prove himself that he truly meant what he said and she duly got on with plucking and preparing the chicken. I asked my mum if I could have a go at plucking the chickens and together outside I starting having a go – I thought it was very easy and it seemed to come to me naturally considering how very young I was at the time, the only thing I did not like was the noise it produced from scragging the feathers off, it sounded like an empty cardboard box; nevertheless, I carried on.

Friday was payday and my father as promised returned on time with his wages so my mother could duly go and do the weekly shopping for the family. One day on a Saturday, he kept badgering her to give him some money as he wanted to go and gamble on the horses, my mother refused to give him the money telling him that she needed what she had left in order to buy more essentials for the week ahead, and then he slapped her so hard across the face, it instantly bruised in the shape of a big hand print. With this she went running out of the house and straight to Mr and Mrs Jones crying and beside herself, telling them what she had been subjected to.

Mr and Mrs Jones could see straight away the severe bruising on her face, they were very sympathetic towards her and liked her very much, but there was little they could do except comfort her and calm her down, giving plenty of reassurance that she could come any time and express her fears and concerns. They certainly did not agree with domestic violence but in those days, there was very little that could be done with regard to marital affairs; the police at that time would never get involved with domestic disputes, no matter how bad things got between a husband and wife.

My father had made our tea; he had us sitting on the floor in the lounge like three little soldiers on parade with our plates in front of us. We were not allowed to touch our food until he gave the order that we could commence eating; even at a very young age I thought this to be very odd, he had us all in a little line according to our age group, the eldest, the second and the third. I was kneeling and he screamed at me to get off my knees and to sit crossed legged like the rest of my sisters. He told me that I was never ever to kneel on my knees ever again because it makes a female have horrible legs in the future; since then I have never kneeled on my knees, something that has stayed with me all of these years.

My mother had returned and came in through the back door which led straight into the kitchen. As soon as my father heard that she was back he bolted into the kitchen, I could hear raised voices and was just too terrified to even try to listen to what was going on. She then quickly came through the lounge with my dad in hot pursuit through to the hallway and the front door. I saw him grab her arms and he was pulling her to the door opening it at the same time, shouting at her and saying he was now taking command of the home and he wanted her out.

I got up and went to the door and starting screaming, "Leave Mummy alone, leave her alone."

At this point I was right behind them and with the front door fully open and with one big push, he threw my mum out of the door with such force that I witnessed her falling straight to the ground head first and flat out on her tummy – she was 6 months pregnant.

He then slammed the door shut and locked it, there was pounding on the door, my mum hysterical, telling him to let her in, my sisters and I were crying and screaming at the top of our voices to let Mummy in, but he took no notice of our plight and told us to get back in line on the floor and he ran into the kitchen to lock the back door. I noticed that he was laughing, finding the whole situation highly amusing as Mum was frantically turning the door knob of the kitchen back door to try and gain entry.

Eventually, when everything fell silent with no more fight coming from her, he unlocked the door and returned to the lounge where we were sitting and started reading the newspaper as if nothing had ever gone on. We were told to pick up our plates and put them in the kitchen.

Mum was sitting near the kitchen table very quiet with tears rolling down from her eyes, she was holding down on both sides of the chair and looked like she was in a lot of pain and very pale and perspiring, I noticed blood on the floor. I immediately went to my father to tell him there was blood on the floor, he then told us to go to our bedroom and stay there and don't come out.

My father had got in touch with our local doctors to come and see my mother as she was bleeding and 6 months pregnant. The doctor came and made an assessment of the situation and made a diagnosis that the pregnancy might be starting to self-terminate. The only thing my mother told the doctor was that she had taken a fall and fell straight onto her stomach; she couldn't tell him anything else in complete fear of what my father would further subject her to. The doctor made recommendations that my mother had to rest and stay in bed for the next few days to see if the bleeding might just stop on its own.

My Aunty Sandra came down to stay to look after my mum and us children whilst my father was out at work; she was my dad's sister. The bleeding had stopped, Mum was up and doing her hair to start her day, my aunty had gone to the shops, I went into my mum's bedroom, she started bending down holding onto her stomach and was now in a lot of pain. She sat down on the bed and was breathing strangely, holding her breath and then breathing again, the pain was coming and going quickly, as she stood up liquid was now on the floor. I was so terrified, I didn't know what was happening with Mum, she said to me, "Val, go and get Aunty Sandra."

I said to Mum, "She's at the shops."

"Go to the white gate and stay there until you see her coming, when you see her tell her to hurry home."

The Ambulance came and Mum was gone. It was many years later I was told that she gave birth to twins, a boy and a girl, Linda and Richard. The boy had died internally and the girl lived for 2 days. In the 1960s there was no chance of survival at the gestational age of 6 months.

My father brutally throwing my mum out of the front door causing her to land on her stomach was what caused her to lose the twins.

The only memory I have of my brother and sister was that fateful day, I always wonder even now what they would have looked like, what would they have done in their lives today.

I found out in my late 20s where they were buried and although I wanted to go and find my brother and sisters' grave, I just couldn't face it, the very thought I found too upsetting.

The twins were never ever talked about again, Mum came home from hospital, the neighbours had bought her a bunch of flowers and a basket full of fruit, I couldn't understand why they had done this. I can distinctly remember the flowers and fruit, I asked my mum why are they giving flowers and fruit but she didn't answer.

Life once again seemed harmonious, Mum and Dad were getting on great and as far as I was concerned, I was enjoying the great feeling of being safe. I soon forgot about the episode of what had happened before, Mum getting thrown out of the family home; my parents looked like they were truly in love, we were the perfect family. And there was news of a new pregnancy not long after the loss of the twins, the only difference being this child was not the result of rape; mum wanted to become pregnant straight away to compensate for the loss of the two children at the hands of my father.

The perfect loving family unit was not to last very long as the erupting volcano of my estranged father's mind was to blow with deadly consequences, a memory that will last forever, scorched in my mind.

October 1965 one afternoon, my father arrived home clutching a long brown holdall where the end of it had been folded over whatever was encased inside, with a light beige combat tie wrapped round over and over again.

I was in the kitchen with Mum and my two sisters were in the lounge playing quietly.

I remember well my father was wearing some type of army canvas jacket, green in colour, and the object that he was carrying he placed on the kitchen table which made a solid thud noise: Mum asked him what the hell it was whilst he was trying to remove his jacket as quickly as possible. And when he did speak, he spoke quickly and breathlessly, he then pulled out of his pocket what looked like a black woolly hat which he also placed on the kitchen table.

He then started to unwrap the object, unwinding the string and holding it in a way that the end of the carrier was still on the table with whatever was inside positioned to slip out onto the table, and that was the very first time I saw with my own eyes the sawn off double barrel shot gun. I really did not know what it was or what it did; uninterested I carried on playing with whatever I was playing with at the time, but I do remember clearly the conversation that took place.

"What the hell are you doing with that in the house, get rid of it, I don't want it in the house, are you listening to me Lou, I don't want it here."

"Oh stop worrying Nancy, it's fine, I need it, I'm just keeping it for when I go pheasant shooting with the guys, stop nagging on woman, I am going to put it away in a minute in a safe place."

My father was then busy going through his jacket pockets and placed a box onto the table and then some other bits which had shiny golding round it in a deep orange red colour, about three maybe four. I of course did not know what these objects were. He opened the box and placed these things within the box that seemed to have separate compartments to accommodate each individual one; it wasn't until years later I got to know that they were shot gun cartridges. He then placed the shot gun back into the brown carrying sleeve and started winding the combat string around it.

My father then went towards the end of the kitchen unit and right on floor level, there was a square flap which he turned upwards towards the left and slid the gun and cartridges in it, then slid the flap over the concealed compartment, not even battering an eyelid that this was all done before my eyes.

Mum was 4 months pregnant with my youngest sister Paula and the last Lawson to be produced. My father as normal had disappeared for a few days and it was getting to the stage that I was feeling happier when he was not around, but one afternoon he came tearing in, and was putting the shot gun back in its hiding place, Mum screaming at him and asking him where the hell had he been for the last few days. His reply was he had been out hunting with his friends.

Mum did not question him any further in front of me, he was acting strange, smoking a lot more than usual and he seemed not to be able to relax, he was up and down, here and there. Mum asked me to go into the lounge which I did straight away, then I heard Mum say to him, "What have you been up Lou? Something has gone on, you better tell me, you better not be bringing the police to this door."

A few days had passed and my father was in all day long, not going out at all; I hated every minute of him being there. I did wonder why he had not gone to work, the home was very quiet and Mum and Dad didn't really say much to each other either.

One morning my father made an announcement that he was quickly popping to the corner shops to buy some tobacco and with that he was gone and out of the back door like a flash. I was relieved as every time he popped out, he would be gone for days or even weeks, I was getting quite used to that. I remember wishing he was gone and never coming back. I felt all light and fluffy, in a sense a feeling like a big burden had been lifted off my tiny shoulders; for a 3-year-old I was very forward for my age and a very deep thinker, always scrambling to make sense of the world that I was encased in.

My joy and inner feelings of being safe and happy with just us and Mum were dashed short, before I even had the chance to enjoy the fact that he was gone my father was back and carrying a bottle.

The house, the family unit had gone back to being subdued with us kids playing quietly in our bedrooms. For some reason, I had an overwhelming feeling of fear, I was unable to relax and enjoy being a child; where my world and my sister's world should have been bright, beautiful and colourful, our world was dark and dismal.

We had our tea at the kitchen table and I could smell the putrid smell of alcohol coming from my father's breath. He was in a joking mood, trying to make us kids lighten up and laugh along with him. He said after tea we would sit down and play Scrabble with him – a 3-year-old, a 2-year-old and a 1-year-old playing the adult game of Scrabble.

"Come on Nancy relax, you can come and play scrabble with us, it will do you good and stop you being chained to that fucking sink."

Mum never said a word and carried on doing the washing up. I remember Mum never sitting at the kitchen table having a meal with us when my father was around; in fact, I don't recall seeing my mum eat anything at all.

We were marched into the lounge and made to sit at the table and my 1-year-old sister Hazel was promptly put at the table in her wooden high chair. I was intrigued as to what this Scrabble was actually about. A board came out with lots of little wooden squares poured onto the table, my father re-arranging them face up with numbers and letters on them and then having a longer piece of wood placed before each of us. My father then putting these little squares on the long wooden block with the letters with the smaller numbers on them. Mum then came into the lounge and said to my father, "Lou how do you think they can play this game with you when they don't even know their alphabet and Val only knows numbers up to 12 and a few letters."

"I will help them with it."

I soon got very bored playing this game and was becoming increasingly frustrated. I wanted to get down and come away from the table and away from my father, it felt like forever, I didn't like the smell of alcohol pouring out from his breath.

Mum entered the lounge and said, "Come on it's time to put it away, the girls have to have a bath and it's time for bed, I am just going to run their bath so put it all away Lou."

That was the most magical set of words I heard that day, saved by Mum, it was the very first time I was actually looking forward to going to bed as normally I would always play up in order to stay up with Mum.

Mum always got Hazel done and dusted first, probably because she was the youngest and me and my other sister shared a bath giving us time to splash around playing with the bubbles and having a lot of fun. But when our father was home this fun was done more quietly, Mum always joined in placing funny shapes made in the bubbles upon our heads.

We were in our pajamas, had brushed our teeth and were having our last cup of milk before we went to bed, and Mum told us to go and say goodnight to our father on the way through. I really didn't want to and made it very obvious in the body language a 3-year-old would display, "Val come on do, what I say darling."

I duly said good night as quickly as I could, making sure I was running through rather than walking – I did not want a kiss from him.

I was cold that night and found it very hard to sleep, my sister was thrashing about, I shared a bed with my sister, top and tail.

Eventually, I could feel myself slipping into sleep holding onto my teddy. I loved my teddy, he was my everything to me and as soon as teddy was by my lips, I would gently start sucking and sleep would always follow.

I started to stir, I wasn't sure what I was hearing and it took me a few seconds to come round from slumber. Then it registered, I could hear my father bellowing at the top of his lungs at Mum; it was another full blown argument; whenever my father was intoxicated with alcohol this would always occur. I was unsure if I should get up and go to where Mum was, my heart started thumping in my chest and my mouth had gone all dry, I really was terrified, there was no movement from my sister, she was still fast asleep.

I got up and made my way to where the arguing was happening, I got to the kitchen door and was standing there holding onto my teddy listening and watching, my parents were totally unaware that I was there. I heard Mum say to my father, "Can I have some money for shopping tomorrow, I need to buy a bag of coal as we haven't got any hot water and I need to get some food in for the children."

My father said, "I haven't got any bloody money, I lost it all on the horse racing."

My mother said, "You blew it all on the horses? What am I going to do now, how am I going to feed the children, I need coal for hot water."

My father said, "You fucking bitch, I told you I haven't got any money, I've fucking had enough of you, I'm going to shoot you." Whilst he was saying that he was bending down to the corner of the kitchen unit and pulling out the sawn off double barrel shot gun.

Mum backed away from the kitchen sink and walked backwards and backed herself against the kitchen wall terrified and screaming at him, "Don't you dare do that, you're drunk and bloody mad."

I started screaming and stood frozen in the doorway holding onto my teddy, my father standing there with the shot gun aimed at my mother's head. He was laughing and swearing, lowering the gun away and then raising it, taking aim at my mother's head, her eyes transfixed on the shot gun, her eyes following every rise and fall, pressing herself harder and harder against the wall, completely rigid with terror.

My whole body from head to toe started shaking taking on a life of its own, I screamed again at the top of my lungs, I let out a loud piercing scream, "No Daddy, no Daddy!" and whilst I said this I ran straight in front of my mum, holding onto her and facing my father with the gun pointed at my mum's head, and within seconds of my movements my father pulled the trigger.

My mother moved her head and body holding onto me as well but, still pinned rigid to the wall, she moved to the right. With a very loud bang and explosion I saw the gun jerk up right with the force of the shot gun going off, there was a massive hole in the wall and a peppering of smaller holes, the kitchen was filled with a smoke with a strong pungent smell of sulphur.

My father grabbed his holdall, put the gun inside and was gone into the night. Mum slipped to the floor still holding onto me and pulling me down with her, both of us crying and in shock. I looked up at Mum and could see bits of wall debris all over her; it was on the floor and even ended up in the kitchen sink.

The next thing I could hear was banging on the front door and a rush of panic footsteps, people rushing in, Mum and myself couldn't move, everything moving in slow motion, I could only see people's faces as a blur, and a constant rewind mode of what had just happened, over and over in my mind, 3 years old, Bang, Bang, Bang.

No Police were called, I remember some lady holding me tight and other people picking my mother up and giving her drink, the rest of that night is a total blank to me.

The next morning I was up, I dragged the kitchen chair to enable me to climb up and look at the hole in the wall; I was fascinated that I could see into the lounge via this hole. I also put my finger into the smaller holes to see what it felt like, still unaware of what really went on.

Before I knew it Mum was there right behind me and she said, "Val, get down from there and don't you ever climb onto a chair on your own ever again."

I said to Mum, "It's a hole, I can see through it."

Mum said, "Yes I know, come on get down, I will have to find a picture to hide it."

Mum did find a couple of cheap pictures in a plastic white frame large enough to cover both sides of the wall, I remember distinctly looking at these pictures and knowing what was hidden behind them.

The events of what happened that night were never spoken of again until 40 years later.

Roughly about two weeks later in the morning, I had just finished my breakfast, Mum had just taken the kettle from the gas stove to make a pot of tea, when there was a massive disturbance with loud banging on the front door and the back kitchen door where we were. I heard a voice saying, "Open up, police."

Mum hurried to the door to open it but just before she had the chance to do so, the door was already busted open and the police were inside; there were loads of them just piling in and totally disregarding us children they were everywhere, looking, searching and rushing around, it was pure chaos.

A couple of these police officers then came back into the kitchen and started questioning Mum asking her when was the last time she had seen her husband and if she knew of his whereabouts, as they were looking for him, a warrant for his arrest was issued.

Mum said, "Why is there a warrant out for his arrest?"

The police officer said, "Because he is involved in an armed robbery, two people have already been arrested and have coughed up who the others were and your husband is one of them. We also know he had a shot gun, so have you seen it or your husband?"

The minute I heard him say this I knew straight away what they were after, I could feel myself looking into the corner of the kitchen unit where the gun was hidden. I remember thinking to myself, don't look there or the policeman is going to know through my eyes that there in the corner is where the gun was hidden.

Mum told the police that she had not seen him in ages and doesn't know anything about any gun or where he could possibly be and that she wanted the police out of her home now. Mum was looking at me in a way that told me, don't say anything. I remember thinking to myself, why is Mum saying that when we have seen Dad and there was a big hole in the wall behind the pictures.

When the police had gone I said to Mum, "We have seen Dad and the gun is hidden in there over there behind the flap."

"No Val, it's gone, your dad has taken it away, look I will show you, but don't tell anybody about this flap, if you do it will just cause trouble and we don't want that do we."

My mum went over to the corner and moved the flap to one side, I went and had a look and saw it was empty, all gone. I did feel relieved as I had become fearful of the noise it created, not that I had any clue that it could have killed Mum or myself; it was only years later that I became aware that I could have stood witness to the murder of my own mum.

50 years on as I write this book it still feels unreal, a dream, a made up story and totally unbeknown to me

that the effects from this incident had already affected me and would be buried deep within my subconscious where I would feel them when I am subjected to a similar incident and faced with a gun aimed at me later on in my life.

Writing this book has been very hard and painful for my mum as she is catapulted back into a very painful and traumatic past that she would rather forget, as it was something she had to deal with on her own. No one to talk to about it, no one to help her and give her understanding; and what makes it even worse, to be ripped away from her family in Kenya never to see her own mother ever again.

53 years ago was the last time Mum saw her mother, the very thought of myself not seeing my mother makes me shudder.

Life again was getting back to normal, just Mum and us, our little unit. I was so pleased that my father had gone and was no longer in our lives. My little sister Paula was born and I loved her and was always playing with her. We are the only ones out of all my sisters that look more like each other.

The 2-bedroom bungalow was feeling crowded and tension was building up in Mum as we were still waiting for our council house. The other neighbours had already been allocated their council homes even though we had been there longer than anyone else. New rough families were moving in with wild kids; the family that had moved in opposite us in the 3-bedroom bungalow had 13 children, and when they came out of their bungalow, they didn't come out, they poured out. Us a little family found them frightening and very intimidating and that's when it all started, the name calling from the children and the parents, "Nigger, nigger, nigger."

I at the time didn't know what these words were or even what they meant but all I do know, is that the whole family were hell bent on saying these words every time they saw us, and even more new words would come out directed at us, "Blacks, blacky, blacky."

I would be playing in our garden which was not separated by any fencing and these wild kids would just walk over into our garden area and say to me, "Your mum is a nigger, black as tar, she is black, black, black, and you are a nigger kid that's what you are, go back to your own country, we don't want black niggers here."

I said to them, "Leave us alone, my mum is not black," and with that one of the boys punched me in the mouth, and all the blood was then on my white top. I started crying and ran inside to tell Mum what they had done to me, and what they were saying, that was the very first time I had been hit, I did not understand why they had hit me, and it would certainly not be the last either.

Mum stopped us from playing outside in order to keep us protected from these really vile people, but it did get me thinking, as I mentioned before even at such a young age; I always thought deeply to try and make sense of the world I lived in. I was 4 years old now and I remember looking at Mum, and for the first time I could see that Mum was a different colour. I did not see any difference before, but it did not make any changes to me so I just shrugged it off, so what, I love my mum.

At times Mum was forced to put washing out on the line and when she did, if the family was about which was most of the time, then my mother would be a target for full racist remarks, the old favourites from the parents, "Fucking Niggers, why have we got to have 'em in our own country, nigger go back home, go back home and swing in your tree, taking up our houses, get back in your mud hut where you belong."

This was becoming a ritual which was starting to upset Mum very much. She used to leave the back door open and I could see and hear all the nasty vile things that were being said to her, and not once did I hear Mum say anything back.

The next course of events that took place was them emptying their bins in our garden which looked like a rubbish tip after they had finished. I watched my mum time after time picking up their rubbish and putting it into our own bin, sometimes I would go out there with her to help make the job a bit easier.

Eventually, this started to have a detrimental effect on Mum and she started suffering with depression and would always be breaking down crying. The doctors put her on anti-depressants, she kept going to see Mr and Mrs Jones asking them to find out why she had not been allocated a council house, they said it would be looked into, even they couldn't understand why we had not been given one.

It was very early in the morning when Mum could smell smoke, something burning. She got up and rushed out to see where the smell of smoke had come from and what she found was shocking; the front door net curtains were on fire and in the letter box was a rolled up, crunched up newspaper that had been deliberately set alight and put through our letter box. I remember her running to get a saucepan full of water and throwing it at the door to put the fire out.

The net curtains were hard and black like burnt plastic and the paint on the door had burnt off a bit as well. This time Mum was really angry and I remember her saying "Those fucking bastards did it, they are trying to burn us out." She cleaned it all up and found a new bit of net curtain to put up on the front door to give us some privacy as the glass at the top of the door was clear so anyone could look through. Mum then said to me to keep my eyes open as they might come and do it again and if I see any fire, I am to let her know straightaway.

One day I could hear something going on with the letter box and I ran as fast as I could and there it was, newspaper scrunched up and in our letter box. I called for Mum straight away to show her that the newspaper was in the letter box but it was unlit. Mum pulled it out and placed it in the bin, she then said, "It's a warning Val, next time it will be on fire," so every night we went to bed, Mum would pull the net curtain up to stop it from catching alight. I, only being 4 years old, still did not really understand the full danger we were in.

One early afternoon as I was walking past the front door, fire was put through the letter box. The net curtain was down during the day and I saw the newspaper put through the letter box and it was already alight, I screamed to Mum, "Fire in the letter box Mum!"

Everything that was happening, the continued bullying, the abuse, fire being put through our letter box was having a detrimental effect on Mum's mental wellbeing; she was already on anti-depressants, so Mr and Mrs Jones decided it was time to contact Social Services so they could step in and help us as a family.

Social Services contacted the Council to try and find out why we were still there and had not been allocated a council house as there had already been families that had only been there a short while and had been offered accommodation before us, considering we were on the waiting list before all of them.

Our situation was causing such great concern to Social Services that they decided we had to move as quickly as possible as our very lives were in danger; the council said that they were not in a position to allocate us a home, the reason being there simply was nothing available.

We moved to Bognor Regis, there was temporary accommodation ready for us. Mum had to leave some of our furniture behind because we couldn't fit it all in the home we were moving to.

I was over the moon with our new home. It was an old Edwardian building that had been converted into two flats, the garden had been left unattended with rubbish everywhere, bits of broken toys, old dolls and this amazing child's umbrella. I was so fascinated by it and played with it all the time, I just loved it when it was raining and would constantly open it up and hold it above my head shielding myself from the rain. The pathway was green and very slippery, everything was covered in this green slimy substance, I would just try and wipe it off and continue playing with the toys that had been chucked out and left there abandoned by their previous owners.

I was 4 years old and the time came that I had to attend school which was just around the corner from where we lived just past the St Mary Magdalene Church, built in 1404, which had a school that was part of the church made out of flint stone, and called the old school house.

I feel very honored and privileged to have attended this school and become part of its history, the old school house is now a Museum of Victorian life built in 1885.

I don't really want to go into the history of the school; even though it is fascinating it would take my reader into a full history lesson. I would like to but feel it would be a book in itself.

The church graveyard that I had to go through every morning was the most terrifying ordeal I experienced as a young 4-year-old child. I remember building myself up mentally to run through the graveyard as quickly as I could in case any lurking monster was ready to get me; the trees and pathway were always dark as not much light could get through, and all the 14th century huge gravestones were just as frightening and intimidating, giving off a warning, come through at your own peril.

I did not have the luxury of being taken to school by Mum, she had my sisters and couldn't get them all up and out in the mornings to get me to school which was just round the corner, neither did Mum have any friends to look after the kids so she could take me to school.

47

My school route never took me off the pathway, I did not have to cross any roads, the pathway only ended at the church, where I had the choice of cutting through the church graveyard or coming off the pathway and out onto the road and Mum told me I was not allowed to come off the pathway.

I never at any time told Mum how terrified I was taking myself to school and having to go through the graveyard on my own. I never at any time recall seeing any of the other school children making their own way either, I was entirely on my own.

I do consider myself very lucky that on the same pathway there was a blacksmiths; I remember always stopping to have a look to see what was going on inside, the minute the doors were open you would be hit with a rush of warm air that would quickly take the morning chill out of your bones.

On this particular morning on my way to school it had been snowing very heavily, and all the snow had frozen solid, it was quite dangerous and slippery. I had never walked in the snow on my own before and I remember that I was very nervous and kept telling myself, you can do it, just walk very slowly and I would be ok the minute I got on the frozen, iced up pathway.

I was slipping and sliding everywhere, I had never had any experience walking on ice before, I was only 4 years old and before I knew what was what, I was on the floor feeling very cold and my woolly tights getting wet. Every time I tried to get to my feet I would hit the ground again. Managing to hoist myself up by gripping onto a wall which was close to the church graveyard, I couldn't move, I wouldn't move, I was so terrified I started crying and whimpering. I was stuck and not going anywhere, until this elderly lady came up to me and asked what was wrong. I told her I was stuck and scared of walking on the ice, I had to get to school, and I remember her taking my hand and telling me not to worry, "I will take you to school." The minute this lady held my hand I felt safe to move, and I remember this old lady having such a kind looking smiley face. In all the times I used the pathway, I never saw this lady ever again.

My time and experience at this one-classroom school was the best school I had ever been to. I was at peace in this school, the teachers were nice and so were the children.

Chapter 2

Hide Away

Valentine's Day 1967 was our moving date into our Council home. Social Services arranged for a removal van to collect our belongings for our new address and Mum paid for the taxi for us to go to Littlehampton.

I remember the day we arrived at our new home. It was a rundown council area, there were no garden fences, and the privet hedges had all been trampled down with just mud patches through the gardens where the grass had died and was being used as a cut through rather than using the proper path ways. Other gardens had old cars with the doors missing, oil patches everywhere, broken up motor cycles, it looked like some rubbish tip to be honest. There were kids running around with craggy looking clothes, wild unkempt hair, rubbish in the streets, dogs roaming everywhere, the worst place anyone could wish to live and that is where we were put.

Our house was a pre-war 3-bedroom semi-detached house with an outside toilet and the bathroom was in the kitchen that was added to at some later stage with a coal house inside the kitchen as well. The old pre-war gas lamp still adorned the kitchen wall and that had just been painted over and was no longer functional.

In all of the bedrooms upstairs, each room had its own inactive coal fires. My bedroom was the back bedroom that I would share with a sister, I looked out of my bedroom window to view our back garden which was huge and very long. You could see that the garden had been unkempt for a very long time as it had taken on a life of its own with wild blackberry bushes looking like triffids, with winding arms twisting and turning choking the life out of the garden and turning onto all the old bits of wood and debris that had been left behind. The back pathway leading to the garden gate that was leaning over on its side was overrun with weeds, stinging nettles and general household rubbish and this was the view to my eyes of our new home, a dump.

I knew straight away I did not like where we had moved to but just had to get on with it. I was unaware of the horrific nightmare that was going to besiege me living here and what trouble lay ahead.

The house was dirty and smelly, and the council had not even bothered painting the house with the magnolia wash that it often did when new tenants moved in, they just left tins of magnolia paint for us to do it ourselves. The house was in a state of disrepair, the tenant that lived there before was an elderly man who had died a few weeks before we moved in. The council disposed of his household belongings and that was it, get the next tenants in regardless of whether or not it was fit for human habitation.

Mum braced herself and got on with scrubbing the walls in the lounge, the hallway and the bare wooden stairs which were black with grime, and there was a pungent stink of cats' urine and tom cat spray. The smell made me feel really sick and the amount of dirty grime I had never seen or been exposed to before in such squalid conditions; I was used to cleanliness which is next to godliness so these conditions were very shocking to me.

As Mum was cleaning and in charge of 4 young children the task ahead was a difficult one. A knock at the front door and our first visitor a neighbour a couple of doors down called Rosy introduced herself to Mum and volunteered to help her with the scrubbing which was very nice; we were not used to anyone even acknowledging that we were alive. Rosy turned out to be a very kind, lovely woman, she had a very large family whose kids were the kids from pure hell, and not long after, Rosy walked out on her kids and family, she just couldn't cope with how dysfunctional they were; she ended up having a serious nervous breakdown.

I was due to start a new school. I had also turned 5 years old and I was looking forward to it.

The school was comprised of new buildings and all flat on ground level. I was taken to my classroom which I thought looked really nice – new and welcoming. I can remember well my first day, it was a bright warm sunny morning and the class had outside activities in the form of water features with old washing up liquid bottles where I could suck up water and squeeze it back out, pouring it over other objects and floating coloured balls in it. I thought it was brilliant and absolutely enjoyed myself; I had never played with water that way before. Just before it was time for our morning break, we all had to go back inside sit down and be given our little bottle of milk that all children got at that time which was free. I liked milk but was very intrigued by the little miniature sized bottle of milk which was the same as the bottles of milk we had delivered by the milkman each morning but those were much larger. After everyone had finished their milk, each of us had to put the empty bottles back into the milk crate and go off to the playground for playtime.

The playground was just a square tarmac area and that was it, children were running around, playing with skipping ropes and generally having a good time. As for me, I didn't know anyone and just walked onto the playground watching and seeing what everyone was doing. I got to just about the middle of the playground when suddenly I was feeling immense pain, some large girl was pounding and thumping me on my back and then the back of my head screaming at me "nigger, nigger." I remember feeling confused and not really understanding for a few seconds what was happening to me. When it finally registered I was being beaten up, my hair was being pulled, causing me to bend over sideways and then all these kicks were being thrown in. I could then hear the school bell ringing and as if by magic, the playground was empty. I was trying my hardest not to cry, I fixed my clothes and went back into the classroom saying nothing and looking at no one.

I was feeling very upset, I did not want to be at this school, I wanted to just go home.

Lunchtime came around quickly and we were told to get into a line, girls in one line, boys in the other. I was reluctant to get up and made sure I got in line at the very end and off we marched, following the teacher into the dining hall. There were lots of tables with cups and jugs of water placed on each table. The children rushed to their tables, I stood still in my tracks until a teacher held my hand and led me to sit at a table with some other kids.

The lunch was bangers, mash and peas with gravy and the teacher placed my plate of food in front of me. I was hungry but just too upset to even think about eating it, all the other children were scoffing it back like no tomorrow. The teacher came over to me and asked why I was not eating my lunch and I simply replied that I didn't want it.

The lunch in the dining room was coming to an end and that meant the playground. I was feeling very nervous and afraid that the large girl was going to get me again, so I waited in the dining room until all the kids had left. I was on my own, something that I was to get used to very fast; being on my own kept me safe from being beaten up and being called these horrible names.

I came out of the dining room and entered a long hallway leading off to all the different classrooms. I could see the shiny floors and could still smell the newness of the building. As I was walking through I could feel myself walking very slowly and keeping myself as close to the wall as I could possibly get, looking all the time for somewhere I could go to be out of sight of the other children, what I was looking for was a place of safety.

I came to the entrance of my classroom and went inside heading to the main outside door, if I turned right that would lead me to the playground, if I turned left that would take me to the outside of the school building. I turned left walking slowly to see if it would lead me to a place of safety. As I proceeded I noticed it took me past the dining room, then a long brick wall, and then in view was the other playground for the older children, then a wooden hut which was a separate classroom. I headed for the wooden hut, behind it rather than the front, the wooden hut was raised and I could see under it, then a big green field that went down as far as the eye could see. This area was quiet, no kids about so perfect to just sit out the playtime and be safe.

I remember sitting down on the grass and trying to lean back against the wooden hut, but that was impossible I was too small and would fall straight under the hut. So what I had to do was raise myself up and lean against the building that way, after a little while, my back would start to hurt but I didn't care, I had to do this to keep myself safe.

Throughout my stay at this school this is where I came every play time, and lunchtime until I eventually left this school for junior school.

The bell rang it was home time, I couldn't wait to see Mum and just get home as fast as possible. I waited until the kids had shot out of the classroom before I made my way out and to spot Mum waiting for me outside, there she was with a big smile on her face, she said to me,

"Come on Val, hurry up, I've left your sisters at home on their own, we need to get back as quickly as possible."

The walk home was less than 10 minutes, we got to the end of the road and there was a Lollipop lady. I had never seen one before, I was totally mesmerized by this lady, I thought it was fantastic that she stopped the traffic to allow us to cross the road safely. I remember that I would keep looking back at this lady in awe of what she looked like and what she was wearing.

As soon as we got through the front door my sisters were excited to see their big sister back home from school and wanted to know how I had gotten on with my first day. I told my sisters about playing with water and coloured balls, and that inside the classroom there was a Wendy house that I played in. I told them about the tiny bottle of milk I was given, but I chose not to tell them about the large girl that had beaten me up.

The next morning Mum came to wake me up to get ready for school. I really didn't want to go, but still I did not say anything to her about being beaten up yesterday. My sisters were still fast asleep so Mum could slip out quickly, get me into school and be back home before they realised she was not there. This particular morning it was cold; Mum had put my woolly tights on. Every time I walked in these tights, the crotch would end up where my knees were, forcing me to walk in penguin mode, and this beige pure wool hat that had side bits to cover your ears would be tied under my chin ensuring that no cold air or wind was going to get in no matter what. I was holding Mums' hand, she was trying to get me moving faster which I found very hard because of what was happening with my tights and to top it all, I was scragging around with my other hand trying to pull off this very irritating pure wool hat that was causing me great discomfort, scratching my skin, making my head very itchy and also creating a massive amount of heat on my head. It was that hot I could have combusted! I could not stand the unpleasant feeling any longer; this hat had to come off as far as I was concerned. Mum caught me tugging at it trying to rip it off and tapped my hand telling me to leave my hat alone. I told Mum that it was horrible – itchy and scratchy and burning my head, Mum still said leave it on.

We arrived at this tiny little alleyway which led into the school grounds and Mum stopped here and told me that I could walk the rest of the way on my own. She gave me a kiss and was gone. In my thoughts I couldn't wait for Mum to be out of sight, I then ripped off the woollen hat and placed it in my school bag; I will never forget the sensation I felt the minute that hat came off, it was like a quick smack of cold air hitting my head. I swear I could see steam rising from my head, but little did I know that I would have to endure this woollen hat for three more consecutive days.

Oh my God I was at the school grounds. I was terrified about where this large girl was going to be and was I going to get what I received yesterday. From the little alleyway, I could peak at the playground; I could see kids there playing and decided to hover about in the alley until I could hear the bell ring to go inside.

I got into my classroom easily enough and headed straight for the toilets to get these woolly tights off. I had never taken tights off before and found it quite a hard job, I was pulling and tugging, I did not care if I was there all day, these tights were coming off somehow. In the end I got my victory, they were off and stuffed into my school bag where they belonged, it was so nice walking normally again and not like some trussed up penguin. As I got into my classroom I scanned the room for the large girl but she was nowhere to be seen.

My days in this part of the school went alright. I was not in fear of the large girl, she was no longer at the school, I did find out when I eventually transferred into junior school where she had gone to.

I kept myself to myself, I did not have a choice really; the children were uninterested in playing with me or even speaking to me, I was there but not recognised in any way shape or form. But at least the racial name calling and being hit no longer occurred, I was grateful for that.

The summer had arrived, this was my favourite time of the year, and every playtime and lunchtime I returned to my hideaway behind the wooden classroom. One day, it was a beautiful day and the green field before me took on a different form. I could see right into the distance, a derelict old farm barn with old equipment to work the land turning over the soil. My back was hurting from staying raised and leaning against the classroom hut, there was a gentle warm breeze blowing on me and this felt really lovely and uplifted my very low spirit from constantly being so lonely at school. The farm barn was beckoning for me to come and explore that area. I thought to myself, would I get into trouble going all the way down there as it was not part of the school grounds. Thinking about it now as I write, it was my small way of thinking someone might have cared.

The field was so lush and green, the sky was crystal blue not a cloud in sight, I started my slow descent towards the old farm barn, enjoying the summer rays pouring onto my skin, I so loved that feeling.

It was amazing the sight of the old rickety barn, there was a disused tractor that was rusted up from being left for a long time and this big wheel type thing with lots of long sharp spokes that I imagine would be attached to the tractor to churn up the soil in the fields. I was looking and going into deep thought on how this machinery would have operated – as I have mentioned before I was always a deep thinker and always trying to process the world I was encased in.

My love of history developed from a very young age, I was fascinated by old buildings and the history behind them.

The summer holidays had arrived, no school for six weeks, and this meant I got time to play with my sisters, and when the holidays were over, I had a sister who would also start at the same school, except I would be at the other side of the school where the older children went before the next stage, junior school.

Us sisters played in the back garden, the back steps really, as the garden had not been tended to, it was still all wild, Mum had enough to get sorted out let alone a woman on her own with 4 small children to be able to clear the garden of all the debris it held.

The back of our house backed onto a huge field which contained at least 4 football pitches and further on was a children's playground which was known as the Rec; it held a large slide, four swings, 3 children's swings and a great big sandpit.

All of us sisters wanted to go over there and play, then came the opportunity. I could see no other children playing at this playground and thought why not, let's go over and play. I asked Mum if it was alright for us to go to the Rec and Mum said it was ok but if there was any kind of trouble, we were to come straight back home.

We were all getting excited as we were getting closer to the Rec, I saw the huge sandpit, never had I seen one before and all I wanted to do was get in it and play.

All of us were jumping in and out, jumping in the sand, pretending it was a swimming pool, we took our socks and shoes off then sat on the edge just sinking our feet into the warm sand feeling it going through our toes, laughing, screaming, making up imaginary games, pretending we were on a pirate ship getting ready to set sail off out to sea.

We were out in the glorious sunshine and having so much fun that none of us saw any kids heading towards us, there were quite a few of them mostly boys, standing around the edge of the sandpit like a pride of lions surrounding their prey with no escape route before they made their kill.

One boy standing out as the leader of the pack started shouting at us saying, "Who told any of you blackies you can play in this sandpit? Fucking get out, you black little niggers."

"Don't you ever get in this sandpit again, it's ours and we don't have black bastards playing with our stuff – it belongs to us."

I could see straight away how scared my sisters were, as they dropped their heads as if they had truly done something wrong. I called my sisters to come on, let's go, and the minute we all got out all the other children piled in the sandpit and started playing, me and my sisters just standing by watching and feeling very sad that our happiness had been so quickly dashed.

I could see all the swings had been taken but the big slide was free, so I beckoned my sisters to make a move for the slide, we could still have some fun on that. I told my sisters that I would have a go first, but just as I was ready to climb the steps, we were surrounded by a pack of kids, the leader of the pack was there again and saying to me "What do you think you're doing?"

I was not sure what I was meant to say except, "I'm having a go on the slide."

The leader of the pack then said, "Get away from that slide nigger, I have told you, no niggers are playing on what belongs to us."

My sisters started whimpering and all of them were scared, the pack of kids then started picking up stones and tossing the stones from hand to hand whilst looking directly at me and laughing. I quickly told my sisters to run home and get Mum.

I could see my sisters in the distance heading for our home, and at this point the kids started throwing the stones at me and picking up more to throw again. There was nowhere for me to go or run to, all I kept doing was walking backwards until I could go no further as I had reached the fence that sectioned off the farm potato field from the playground area. I remember seeing this boy come forward and then throwing this stone at me which hit me square in the middle of my head, it made a heavy thud and vibration noise and everything went black.

I came to with this doctor looking at my head and then putting iodine on it as there was a little hole with a full golf ball sized lump to accompany it.

When I was at home the police came to see me to find out if I knew which child had done this. I could not identify who had done it, just a boy that stepped forward from a lot of other boys; I had never seen these boys before.

The new rules were that we did not go over to the Rec and just played in the garden by the steps or in the field at the end of our garden. I remember so many times looking over at the Rec and seeing all the kids playing, having such a wonderful time and thinking how unfair it was.

The field use to be cut on a regular basis and a man use to go round the field with this little machine that he pushed along creating white marks to mark up the football pitches; I found watching him so fascinating. And when the field had been cut I was in my element, gathering up the cut grass and making the shape of some sort of boat to get inside and play, sometimes my sisters would join in and play pretend games with me.

One time I gathered up the cut grass and made a circle, I then got in it and just laid back looking at the sky and going deep in thought, watching the clouds passing by and asking myself, why am I here, again trying to make sense of the world that I was encased in.

I went on a journey on the train with Mum to Lewis Prison. I have no recollection of attending this prison with Mum, but I do remember coming back on the train from somewhere. When Mum boarded the train one of her high heeled shoes fell off and went under the train. I was eager to climb down under the train and retrieve Mums' shoe for her, this was out of the question. I begged Mum to let me get it totally unaware how dangerous it could be for me, but Mum was so upset, I just wanted to help her.

A train guard walked past and Mum explained what had happened with her shoe, he told her not to worry as he would get it before it was time for the train to pull out of the station.

Not long before, maybe a couple of weeks earlier my father had returned home; he had been gone for a long time, I hated the fact that he had come back into our lives.

Things started changing about the house, my father decorated throughout with wallpaper, and the top half of the garden got tended to, although the bottom half of the garden was left as it was, an absolute mess still with debris everywhere.

A shed had been erected made by my father, a home job, DIY, having robbed the materials from the building site, to accommodate the huge shed he had built – it certainly was an eyesore.

Not long after this shed was built, every weekend my father would make me and my sisters go into the shed, he would lock us in putting a chain and padlock on so we couldn't get out. I didn't really take much notice at first, as I was excited about being in the shed conjuring up in my mind what games we would play. My sisters started crying they were cold, hungry and very bored, we were all bored, but there was nothing more to play. I tried to open the door to come out, but the shed door only opened a little crack, I could see the chain, we were locked in. I tried to make sense as to why the chain had been put on, I could not find any understanding of any of it, so I just sat back down with my sisters and started crying with them. It was now starting to get darker and we could just about still see each other when suddenly I could hear the chain being taken off, my father opened the door and we just marched out went indoors had our tea. Nothing was said, not even an explanation as to why we were locked up in the shed for all of the day.

I found out 50 years later from Mum, that my father locked us in the shed so that he and Mum could go to the pub for the day. There was nothing Mum could do about it, and even if Mum tried, she would put herself at risk of some serious brutal damage; in those days a wife simply obeyed what her husband told her to do.

Sunday morning we were up early and had our breakfast, my father told us to get some toys to play with and get our coats on. I could not understand why we had to put our coats on, maybe we were being taken out, how wrong I was. My father opened the back door and led us to the shed, not saying a word we went inside the shed and the same thing happened again, the chain and padlock was put on. We endured another full day stuck in the shed, this time we did not cry as crying was a waste of time and did nothing to help us with the situation we found ourselves in, we just had to shut up and wait until we were let back out again.

The same procedure occurred; I could hear the chain coming off and my father opening the door to let us out with not one word spoken to us.

We all started retracting into ourselves, like little snails going back into their shell for self-protection; we only spoke to each other, one sister started acting very strangely, she would no longer play anymore and got into a ritual of being on her knees and commenced a rocking motion, forwards and backwards with her head hitting the wall not hard, this then progressed. Her rocking motion developed into her hitting her head on her bed pillow, she would do this continually in her bedroom, it was driving us absolutely mad, I had no understanding why she had the need to do this. One day I tried to physically stop her, by holding onto her, the more I tried the harder she rocked with force against me trying to hold her still. This also progressed to bedtime, the raising of her head up and down on her pillow, my youngest sister calling out to Mum saying she is banging her head on her pillow again.

We did not ask any questions of Mum about why we were locked up in the shed. I had noticed that Mum was not her normal self and was back on the anti-depressant tablets as one time I was in Mum's bedroom, I came across the tablets and opened a capsule to see what was inside; just white powder came out.

My father was back at work, baking bread, wages were coming back into the family household and again my father pulled the same stunt he always did, payday and no sign of him.

I was up sitting in the lounge with Mum watching television, when suddenly there was all this noise, and my father came crashing through the front door absolutely drunk, he was so drunk he couldn't even stand up properly. The lounge door was flung open with my father falling into the lounge and there again this thick putrid smell engulfing the lounge air like some dense fog, the smell of alcohol. My heart was pounding and I froze with fear remembering what happens to Mum when my father was in this state. He was talking, laughing, shouting, the words that came from his drunken mouth were not decipherable, he might as well have been speaking in another language, the language called drunken.

My father then attempted to go upstairs to Mum's room – he just about made it. Mum shot up the stairs to see what he was doing, I followed her and heard her say to my father, "Lou, that's not the toilet, it's my wardrobe." He had urinated in Mum's wardrobe and crashed on the bed, out for the count.

Mum asked me to help her get his shoes off which I did, and Mum managed to get his clothes of throwing his trousers on the floor and then asking me to go through his pockets to see if he had any of the wages left. All I found was some loose change from his pockets and that was all, all the wages had been blown on drink.

The next few days were very quiet and we just stayed and played in our bedrooms.

I remember looking out of the front bedroom window, watching the kids playing out in the street, thinking to myself how lucky they were, playing, laughing and having such a good time, wishing I could be part of their play, maybe one day I thought to myself.

There was not much talk between my parents; my father was out going to work, and once again trying to stick to his broken promises by bringing in a wage on payday Friday.

Saturday had come, I did wonder if we were going to spend the day locked up in the shed, but we were allowed out in the back garden, this time no shed lock up, so we made the most of our freedom and enjoyed playing quietly. My sisters started talking to the children that lived next door through the fence as they too were playing in their gardens.

Sunday, it was an overcast day for the summer, and looked like we were going to get rain and thunder, maybe some lightening which I loved; I thought it was great, to me in my mind it was heaven and the angels deciding to make a noise to let everyone know that they were about.

We had our breakfast and Mum was in the kitchen peeling vegetables, preparing for the Sunday roast. Then my father told us to go and get some toys and get our coats; we knew straightaway what was going to happen, in the shed day.

I and my sisters started crying, going upstairs to get our toys and coats, we really did not want to go into the shed anymore. As we arrived in the kitchen all ready with toys and coats on crying, our eyes out looking at Mum saying we don't want to go back in the shed, Mum said to us,

"Who said you were going in the shed?" My father appeared saying that he wanted us to go and play in the shed, so he could get some peace and quiet and also that Mum could have a break whilst doing the Sunday dinner.

Mum completely went mad at my father; this was the first time I had seen her stand up to him. With a quick snap Mum told my father, "My children are not going in that shed anymore, it's bloody cruel and evil, you listen good Lou, I don't care what you do to me, but my children are staying here with me in the house."

My father did not utter a word, Mum told us to take our coats off and go and play.

I heard Mum say to my father, "You ever put the children in the shed again, I swear to God, I will get a hammer and break that bloody shed."

The summer holidays seemed to have come to a very quick ending. I was looking forward to my sister starting the same school as me, and on our first day my father took us to school.

I was still being ignored as if I wasn't alive, but that really was not a problem, as long as I wasn't being beaten up, or having those horrible names directed at me, all was well.

My sister was in a different part of the school to me, I had moved onto the part of the school for the older children with the other playground.

Just before playtime as usual, we had our miniaturized bottle of milk and then out onto the playground; my new classroom door opened straight onto the playground so I was left with little choice but to go there. I as normal waited for all the kids to leave the classroom before I made my move to try and quickly slip out and off to the hideaway.

When I got outside I was frozen to the spot, I couldn't move in absolute terror, standing there before me was the leader of the pack from the kids over the Rec; I was like a wild animal that freezes to the spot on a road with the oncoming car lights beaming at me, blinded and terrified to make any kind of move in any direction. Lifting his arm up and pointing his finger at me he screamed, "Niggerrrrrrrrrrrrr, I'm going to get you."

I started to push myself hard against the classroom glass windows, praying he would just go and leave me alone. I was trying to merge with the windows so he would not see that I was there, then a couple of other boys appeared from the Rec as well, he pointed me out to the other boys and they started laughing and showing me their fists, that I was going to get it soon and with that they went off to go and play football. I walked slowly looking around all the time to make sure that the boys did not see me going to my hideaway.

6 years old at the hideaway and I was in absolute panic stations, physically shaking in my boots where I stood. I waited there until I heard the bell ring to end playtime, walking to the edge of the wooden hut classroom, to get a view that all the kids had gone. I quickly slipped out and made my way into class.

In class we all had to put these plastic aprons on as we were having a painting lesson. I was so nervous I just couldn't concentrate on what I was supposed to be doing; I loved painting, but my mind was so occupied by what I knew I was going to receive soon, my little brain had entered scramble mode.

After my day back at school getting ready for the home time bell, this time I shot of out the door first and ran to the other side to be there for when my younger sister came out. I knew my father was going to be waiting for us outside, my sister came out all happy, she had had a fabulous first day and was walking out with the girl who lived next door to us. My sister had a friend, which was a great relief to me, as I had been worrying about her all day; with me being in the other part of the school, we were not allowed in the first playground for the new pupils.

My father was there waiting for us, no smiles greeted us from him at all, he did not even ask how our day went. I preferred Mum meeting us, at least she was pleased to see me and always had a lovely smile. It was getting close to the stage of myself disliking this man immensely, I could not hate him as I did not know what hate was, I just wanted him to go away and never come back.

Going to school was causing me great anxiety, trying my hardest to make sure the leader of the pack never clapped eyes on me again and with a little bit of luck, he would soon enough forget all about me. I did manage to do this successfully but it still did not remove the stress of it all, I also had to cope with what was happening at my home; I was living with stress there as well. There was no hideaway; I just had to learn to cope with whatever was going on as far as my father was concerned, a lot for such a young child to carry on such tiny shoulders.

Mum had managed to force my father to rip the shed down and much to my delight the monstrosity, our little jail was gone and no more.

Whilst my father was still with us, we were never allowed to go outside and play, we were limited to the back garden or the house or our bedrooms only, period.

I remember one Saturday early, we went downstairs for our breakfast; the house was quiet and not much being said from anyone. We had our washes and got dressed, my father told us to go upstairs and play in our bedrooms. My father was following us upstairs, then he stopped us going into our own bedrooms, he said he wanted my baby sister Paula in my bedroom with me. I thought this was strange as Paula was not the sister I shared my bedroom with; Hazel and my other sister were in the other bedroom.

I went inside with my little sister Paula and then the bedroom door was closed shut. Again I could not understand why the door was being shut, as the bedroom door was never ever closed at any time. I did not think any more about it and just got on playing with my toys, Paula did the same.

I was starting to get very bored, I had played as much as I could, Paula said she wanted to go and have a wee, so I went to open the door to find that it would only open a little crack. I put my fingers in between the crack and started pulling, there was resistance. I managed to wiggle the door enough to be able to see why the door was stuck, what I found still has me in complete and utter shock today with no understanding. I found that a rope was tied to the door knob. I closed the door shut and told Paula that she had to hold on and try and wait until our father came back to let us out. I told Paula that there was a rope tied to the door to stop us from getting out, which meant we were not allowed out.

A bit of time had passed and Paula could not hold out any longer and started crying as she really needed to go to the toilet, so I immediately started wiggling the door even more and just managed to squeeze through with Paula following as well. My other sisters started crying as they wanted to go to the toilet and also needed to have a drink of water. I managed to get their door opened a crack so both sisters could squeeze through, when I say squeeze through that is exactly what I mean. It took a little bit of time for Hazel and my other sister to squeeze through, we were all free then headed downstairs to go to the toilet. I called out for Mum, no answer. I looked in the lounge no one was in. It then dawned on me that my sisters could not go to toilet because the toilet was outside the back door which was locked, so I told my sisters to use the bathroom and wee in the bath which we all did, and to get a drink of water from the bath taps. I could not make out or understand what was going on, but what I did know for sure that if we were caught being out then we would all be in serious trouble that much I did manage to work out. I ran the bathroom tap for a little while to get rid of any trace of urine, why I did this automatically I couldn't answer I just knew I had to do it.

We all went back upstairs to our bedrooms each one of us repeating the process of squeezing back through the door.

I worked out there was a longer piece of rope hanging down that I could pull down, making the crack close back up with enough room to push the rope back through the tiniest crack and no one would know we had got out.

I sat on my bed deep in thought again trying to make some sense of it all; the rope was tied to my other sisters' bedroom door knob and pulled tight to my bedroom door knob with a longer bit of rope that would be pulled down pulling both doors closed against each other.

A considerable amount of time had passed since we all got out, I could hear Hazel crying and whimpering in the bedroom and my other sister was back to rocking and banging her head on the wall, so I wiggled the door again and squeezed out with my sister Paula. We went into the other bedroom to give my two other sisters some kind of comfort, and when we were all together we all started laughing, giggling and hugging each other and started playing again all together, still not grasping what was happening to us and we certainly did not have anything to be laughing about either. But that is how it was.

We played and played, a lot of time had gone by and it was starting to get dark and still no sign of anyone in the house, so we thought it best to go back into our own bedrooms. But what happened was that my baby sister Paula stayed in her own bedroom that she shared with Hazel, and my other sister came back with me into the bedroom she shared with me. I followed the same procedure and pulled the rope down to re-tie the doors and squeezed the rope hanging down back through the crack of the door. It was quite dark now, so I put the bedroom light on, I got on my bed and just waited. Eventually the doors were untied and the door swung open and that was it, I rushed through and saw my father heading down the stairs, not one word did he utter.

Like a group of little animals set free we were unsure as what to do next, do we stay where we are, or do we go downstairs. We went downstairs and just sat down at the table and said nothing and waited for our tea to be given to us. It really was a strange atmosphere, no words were exchanged between my father and mum, and nothing came from me or my sisters, I never mentioned anything about this until 50 years later.

When I told my mum that we were tied in our bedrooms with rope, no toilet bucket and with nothing to drink, Mum found it hard to believe. Mum said that my father had told her that they would be under an hour going out, and that he had left the toilet bucket on the landing and that he had left drinks, telling us they were popping out and would not be very long. Mum said that she did not see any rope, even though he went straight upstairs, and that she was very upset that they had been gone a long time, but was too afraid to say anything as my father had been drinking all day. This explains why there was no exchange of words between them that evening. I decided not to go further into the rope business as I could see that Mum was in great distress; as far as I was concerned, Mum had been through a lot of painful times, I had survived the experience, so have my sisters, I did not want Mum to go blaming herself for the horrific situation me and my sisters endured.

I did not think any more about the bedroom doors being tied together. It's amazing really, things happen to children they cope at the time forget and move on, but the mind never forgets and stores the information in the back of the subconscious to be retrieved at a later date for analysis and understanding of the incidences labelled out of place.

Once again my father had jumped ship and gone, no signs of him on payday, Mum left to cope again with no money and 4 young children.

Months and months had gone by with no sign of my father, out of sight out of mind, I never thought about him again.

My sister Hazel was now old enough to start school, Mum was in a bad way with her depression and nerves and just about functioning. I took my sisters to school and showed my younger sister which classroom she had to go into, my other sister knew where her new class would be, then all of a sudden, there was no classroom for me to be in. I went to my old classroom and there were new children in there, I did not recognize any of them.

Left outside with no place to go I started crying and went to the first playground where there was a grass mound. I went there and laid on the grass and started sobbing my heart out, then suddenly I heard a woman's voice say to me, "Are you alright, whatever is the matter?" I looked up through my very teary eyes and recognised this lady as Yvonne who lived a few doors down opposite where we lived.

I said to her that I didn't know where I was supposed to be, Yvonne then said to me, "You should have started junior school today, why hasn't your mum taken you there? Come on, I will take you there now."

Chapter 3

Wogamatter

My new school was huge with two playgrounds, one of the playground areas was adorned with five old army air raid shelters made out of bricks with tin corrugated iron roofs. The school used these air raid shelters for storage of school desks and chairs that were neatly packed in them in an orderly fashion.

I remember my teachers' name Miss Lowell; she was an elderly lady who took us for all our lessons for the first year I was there. My classroom was very big and Victorian looking with high arched windows the kind you would see in churches and great, big, huge radiators painted in a thick brown paint. The heat that came from these radiators was immense.

I did not recognise anyone from my infant school, so again I was very much on my own.

The playground was big with so many children playing in it like ants running around busy, not taking any notice of what was going on, spilling on top of each other. I found this so frightening, I decided to walk along the edge of the playground putting one foot in front of the other as if I was marking up in feet the length of where I was walking, keeping my head down and carrying on with the fashion I thought was good enough to use up the play time mode. I looked up when I was at a far distance on the edge of the playground and noticed building men working on a new school. I stood still watching quietly as they were erecting walls with new bricks.

It felt like a very long, lonely day at my new school, and I could feel that I was getting very stressed and worried as I did not know the way back home. I remember constantly trying to remember the way back to my infants' school; once I found that then the rest was easy.

By now my hair was very long. Mum had put my hair in two pigtails with lovely deep navy blue ribbons and I loved it and thought it looked nice. But the only thing I did not like was that Mum had made the pigtails so tight that every time I bent my neck down, I could feel the strain pulling at the nape of my neck causing a stinging sensation.

Nobody spoke to me in my classroom, all the children seemed to be in pairs. I had a desk to myself with the second space being empty.

I did try to make eye contact with the kids in my class in the hope that maybe one just one, would want to become friends with me, but that was never going to happen.

Home time bell started ringing, so I thought I would watch and see where the other children went and maybe this would lead me to the main gates. So I followed the rest of the kids and to my joy and relief I recognised where I was and remembered coming down this long muddy alleyway.

Everyone was in a great rush to get into this alleyway, some kids running, and some pushing and shoving past me. I could now see the posse of kids in the distance, some turning left and some going right at the top of the alleyway. I was unsure of which way I had to go until I arrived at the end myself. Standing still for a moment I looked right and left to see if I could remember anything from when the lady walked me up in the morning, and in the far distance I could just about make out the edge of the infants' school, so I then knew that I had to take a right and just carry on walking all the way down.

I started crying and whimpering with such relief that I knew my way home; I was feeling so lost and at panic stations, I did not care who heard me or even who saw me.

I could then hear hurried footsteps behind me, and looking behind me I could see a number of scruffy looking boys, they started laughing and sniggering at me saying, "Ah Wogamatter, what's wrong with the golliwog." By now these boys were at the side of me, pushing me, putting their feet in front of my feet to try and trip me up, then shoving me into the wall of people's houses as I was passing; this made me cry even more, the kids then went into a chant,

"Wogamatter, Wogamatter oi, oi, oi." The next thing a lad said to me was, "Golliwog, get back on your jam jar, who told you to get off," the laughing and jeering getting louder and louder. I stopped in my tracks and stood still unable to walk forward anymore, I was absolutely terrified.

A lad with short dark, cropped hair and a very freckled face decided that he would start giving me a good kicking with his boots, his feet were everywhere making hard contact with my body. He kicked me up the backside right where the coccyx is, that was so painful, on the legs, and the more his friends egged him on the more and faster he kicked. He then started bouncing up and down like he was a professional kick boxer, laughing and loving every moment of his strength and guts and putting in the most ferocious kicks he could to impress his friends. With that they all ran off laughing at what they had done.

It was so painful and I had to continue standing still, I could not move because of the amount of pain I was in, but knew I had to get home.

I managed to get to the top end of my street, and there waiting for me was the bunch of lads, I heard them say, "There's the black Wog," and I noticed one of the lads was holding onto a ginger haired dog by the collar. This dog was on its hind legs barking and snarling, and trying to make a charge in my direction, with the lad pulling the dog back. I could not even get down my street to have access to my home, so I carried on walking past the entrance to my home and thought it would be safer for me to go the back route into the football field and home through the back garden. My heart was smashing through my chest, my mouth had gone totally dry, and my breathing had become very laboured, I was so scared.

At last I was at the back garden gate and had to be careful to miss the stinging nettles to get through.

I did not say anything to Mum about being kicked, or that she should have known that I was at a different school. All I said was that I had been called horrible names and that Yvonne from across the road took me to my new junior school. Mum said that nobody told her about the new school, all I cared about was I got home alive.

The next morning Mum was up early, all three of us ready for school with my little sister Paula in her pushchair. Great I thought, Mum was taking us to school, my two sisters dropped off at the infants' school, then the long walk to my school; it was so nice having Mum take me, even though I had to show her the way.

Mum said to me that I would have to walk back home by myself, that was not too hard as I knew my way back.

My day at school was a repeat of yesterday, on my own Billy no mates. I moved around the school in break times to give myself the opportunity to explore my surroundings.

I came across the school basement boiler room and I went inside; it was very noisy a bit dark but enough visibility visible to be able to see what was down there and, it was warm. I proceeded to look and see if there was anywhere I could sit down and stay out of site for the duration of the lunchtime mode, most importantly, I wanted it to become another hideaway for safety and protection away from the horrible children that plagued my life with the utmost misery and physical pain, but no chance. It was too noisy and it got to the point that my ears started ringing, and so I would have to continue looking for a safe haven.

Eventually I did find that place of solace and I loved it. On the school grounds they had a big wooden hut which was a classroom all on its own especially provided to accommodate the remedial children of the school and also for children experiencing trouble in their home life with involvement with the police, juvenile courts, social services and so forth.

I was fascinated how different the classroom was. It was adorned with a full sized kitchen with children baking cakes; and the main room looked like a nursery with lots of toys and painted pictures all over the walls, and a wooden work bench with children making bird tables.

Behind this classroom it backed onto a cows' shed with lots of cows in it mooing away, and there was a green railing that I could stand on where I could see the cows getting on with eating their feed and sloshing around in the mud with their big brown eyes focused on me, wondering why is this child standing there looking at them. This is where I came during the play and lunchtime mode, and I did not have a clue that most of the cows in this shed were at their last dropping off point before they were led to the slaughter house. The cows would be there for a few days and then it would be empty which upset me as I had named the individual cows as they were my friends. There was one cow who was brown and white, I called her Dolly. She would walk over to me and allowed me to stroke her, which was quite a stretch for my arms to reach her over the wall.

A new batch of cows came in but they were not as friendly as the cows before, to be honest these cows seemed to have fear in their eyes and certainly took no notice of me what so ever.

On one occasion I came to look at the cows and the local farmer appeared known as John: everyone in the whole town knew John the farmer. He said hello to me and asked me what I was doing there and I told him that I had come to watch the cows but there are no cows in at the moment. With that he smiled at me and walked away, and it must have been about 10 minutes later that John was there bringing in the next lot of cows. So from now on every time I was there and John came along it was a smile and a quick hello; this made me feel happy and special that John the farmer would say hello and give me a smile.

I came to this place very often whether there were cows in it or not. For me I would find that I just stood there staring into space and thinking about absolutely nothing. It was the only place that I felt safe and not have the constant worrying of what was going to happen to me from the kids or my home life.

A new child had come into my class, she was an American girl called Jennifer, and at long last I had made a friend. Jennifer now occupied the empty desk space which felt great, we would be constantly chatting, laughing and getting on with our work together. I was utterly captivated by how she spoke; I did not know what an American was, let alone where America is. The only thing I knew was that she had come to England on an airplane and that she had her own front door key to let herself in as her father was a doctor and never at home when school ended; Jennifer only had to wait about half an hour before her father was home.

Morning breaks and the lunchtime mode, there was me on the playground with Jennifer and now another girl called Linda who had also made friends with Jennifer and now Linda wanted to be friends with me as well; life was beginning to be much better. I was very happy with my 2 new friends.

Linda was a very pretty girl with long blonde hair with the most piecing bright blue eyes I had ever seen; they were so bright and striking you just couldn't help but keep looking at them.

One morning break the three of us were standing at a wall in the playground just chatting and enjoying our break time when a bunch of kids came upon us and starting asking Jennifer and Linda what they were doing hanging around with a nigger. Upon hearing these words from the children, my soul and very being hit the floor with an almighty crash, I did not know what to say, I felt so embarrassed and actually ashamed of myself.

Jennifer and Linda fell silent and did not utter any words our happiness so suddenly dashed, and for the rest of the day the incident left me in deep thought once again trying to make sense of the world I was encased in. At the home time bell, Jennifer and myself headed for the main gates to go home but made sure we stopped outside Linda's classroom so that we could end our school day together. Jennifer and Linda were chatting, and I distanced myself away from any kind of involvement of chat with them, my spirit was very low and I felt kind of crushed really.

When we reached the main gates getting ready to say goodbye and go our separate ways home, Jennifer suddenly blurted out asking Linda and me whether we would like to come to her home for tea. She said that she would ask her father and let us know tomorrow. Well that certainly lifted up my little spirits, I couldn't wait to go to Jennifer's house for tea. We all said goodbye and see you tomorrow, and I headed for the muddy lane to make my descent home. I was feeling very strange inside, a wave of emotion hit me hard like a runaway train smashing me straight to the floor. I felt a lump in my throat as if someone had hold of me by the throat and wouldn't let go, and then the tears started rolling down my face. I remember asking God why is this all happening to me, what had I done that is so wrong.

I reached the end of the alleyway and took my right turn as normal walking down the pathway in a complete daze in a world of my own, when suddenly I could feel hands smashing something down on my head which immediately gave off a pungent smell causing a reaction of vomiting violently. I could hear the kids laughing and running away, and every time I tried to regain my posture from being bent over I would be hit by this pungent smell causing me to vomit all over again. Through watery eyes I could see on the ground in front of me broken up blue with brown speckles – blackbird eggs. There had been quite a lot of these eggs smashed into my hair, and the smell of these eggs were so strong that I was feeling very ill. Every time I tried to walk and get myself home the stiffening smell kept making me retch all the time, I had no more solids in my stomach as I had already emptied my tummy from the vomiting, I was feeling dizzy and also very panic-stricken.

A lady called Kim who came from Burma witnessed the whole thing – she lived in the same street that I lived in – and she took me home and spoke to my mother, relaying everything to her that she had seen the kids do to me and that she knew exactly who they were. Kim helped my mother wash my hair and found it quite a struggle to remove the egg shell that was still permanently stuck to my hair, with the smell causing Kim and Mum to be sick themselves but after 5 washes, it was all removed pungent smell as well.

I had survived the attack, but was left very shaky and nervous, I put the experience to the back of my mind the best way I could.

The positive thing to come out of my attack was that Mum had made a good friend in Kim that lasted years, I liked her very much and she was a friend to me as well.

I went to Jennifer's house for tea along with Linda, I had such a wonderful time; her father was very nice as well and made me feel very welcome in his home. I was so intrigued with Jennifer's stories about her experience on the big plane and how many hours and hours it took her to get to England. I remember wondering to myself, I wonder what it's like being high up in the sky, Jennifer then adding that the airplanes have toilets as well. She then got up and went straight to a draw in her bedroom and produced these miniaturized bars of Camay soap and she gave two to Linda and two to me. Well I was over the moon, I thought these bars of soap was better than bread and butter, anything in miniature size I would always like, and this has carried on into my adult life. All was well with the world until Jennifer delivered a devastating blow to Linda and myself that she only had 2 more months to go and then they would be returning home to America.

I started counting the weeks and then the days and before I knew what was what Jennifer was gone. Never to experience her friendship ever again, I made myself a promise, one day when I grow up I will go to America, I might not see Jennifer but I would be in her land.

It was getting close to the summer holidays 6 weeks off school, and I couldn't wait to spend time with my sisters playing in the back garden and occasionally going over to the Rec if it was empty of course.

I kept a close eye on the Rec to see when it was free so my sisters and I could go and play on the swings and especially the huge sandpit, but every time I looked no chance, it was buzzing with kids all the time.

I was starting to become very bored with the restricted limited area I was forced to play in. I was up in my sisters' bedroom the front bedroom looking out onto the street watching the children playing when I noticed the boy with the short dark hair and freckles on his face; it was the same boy who was bouncing up and down like some kick boxer champion and who gave me that terrible kicking trying to impress his friends.

I ran straight downstairs to tell Mum that the boy was out there in the front who gave me a good kicking and Mum said, "What boy that has given you a kicking?" I then told Mum what he had done and she was furious, she grabbed my hand and led me straight through the front door and right up in front of the boy, Mum then said, "Tell me again what this boy did to you?" I repeated in front of the boy what he had done, Mum then said to me, "I can't fight your battles for you, you have to learn to stick up for yourself, now go and smack him."

I was hesitant and the boy said to me, back in his bouncing kick boxing champion mode, "Come on nigger, what you scared of."

I let rip, I smacked him back, and I lost control and beat the crap out of him with all the other children standing there just watching. After I had finished I just went home, I was shaking in my boots terrified that he would get me later without the support of Mum standing there.

Mum then said to me, "If you don't start protecting yourself and fight back, you will always have bullies picking on you."

That lad never bothered me ever again and the only thing that came from that event was that some of the children that lived in the street wanted to be friends with me. I told Mum that these kids had asked me to come and play with them in their garden, but Mum did not want me mixing with these particular kids as they were a lot older than me and they were trouble and always having the police at their door, with some of the other siblings being taken into care because of their delinquent behaviour.

I took no notice of what Mum relayed to me, as far as I was concerned I was going to be friends with them and be accepted into their gang. And that is exactly what it was, a gang of trouble who broke the law. Little did I know at the time that my life at the age of 7 years old was going to spiral out of control and have me delivered into ultimately the hands of the law and into the Juvenile Court system.

Chapter 4

Delivered into the Hands of the Law

Early in the morning I slipped out of my home and met up with the gang, they were mostly boys – all brothers with one sister Susan who was five years older than me, the brothers ages ranged from 17 years, down through 16, 15 and 14 years, a lot older than me who was only 7 years old, nearly 8, but I was very forward for my small years, I didn't care, all I cared about were that they were my friends regardless.

The oldest lad said, "Come on let's go, we will go to the bullocks field."

I was excited to get going, so off we went, the whole bunch of us. Anyone looking would have automatically thought that we were all trouble makers and regular lawbreakers, little did I know that I was going to enter into a life of crime.

I was absolutely elated with feelings of being accepted, I was part of the human race, I had friends.

We came across a building site near a place called Brooklands Park with a children's playground and thoughts of my sisters immediately sprang to mind. I would bring them to this park where they would be free to enjoy the facilities it provided and without the taunts and racial abuse that we were all subjected to at the rec.

It was a very hot day and I was so thirsty that my mouth had gone all dry and my mind was hell bent on reminding me that I needed to have some water.

The older boys said, "Let's go and check the building site out."

I had never been on a building site before and was eager to see what this new adventure would be all about. We ended walking up this stony, dusty lane that took us behind the building site, there was a lot of activity, with diggers and trucks moving about and workmen going up and down ladders carrying bricks, concrete cement mixers churning round very busy. At that time the workers did not wear hard hats or protective clothing, and most of the workers had no tops on and you could see how red and sunburnt their torsos had become.

A wooden shed had been spotted by the older boys and we were told to go behind the shed which was a tight squeeze as the shed was hard up against the bushes. But we all managed to squat down between the shed and the bushes. I remember feeling excited doing this; it appeared that we were now spying on what was going on at the building site.

Simon then said to all of us, "Stay here, I'm going to go and have a look and see what's inside," and before I knew what was what, he was back in a flash panting in between breaths, trying to relay what he had found. "Fucking hell, there is a large tray of wages in there."

Tom, who was the eldest, then said, "Let me go and have a look, you lot just stay there and be quiet."

It seemed like Tom had been gone for ages, Simon was getting impatient and was just about to make his move back into the shed when Tom was back with the tray of wages in his arms.

I saw packets and packets of these wages, Tom and Simon then started grabbing them out of the tray and stuffing as much as they could into their trouser pockets in the front and the back, in their socks and down the front of their trousers. A few packets were thrust at the rest of us, everyone was moving quickly, squealing, laughing, excited not believing their luck. I did not have any pockets in my light summer dress, so I was at a complete loss as to where I would be putting these two wage packets thrust at me. Then all of them shouted, "Stick 'em down your knickers and fucking leg it."

I had never run so fast in my life before, my heart was pounding, my legs had turned to jelly and I was trembling at the same time I was running, but most of all I liked the feeling it was creating, totally unaware of what I had just become involved in.

We got back to Brooklands Park, the two older lads found a stone built water pump in a small building and the only way we could get in was to go under where a stream of water was running. One by one we disappeared under and into this water pump station in the grounds of Brooklands Park.

There and in privacy everyone was pulling out the wage packets from their pockets and where ever else they had managed to stuff them, ripping them open, there were twenty pound notes, ten pound notes, fivers and loose change. I pulled my wage packets out, I had the same in my packets, but I could not put the loose change back into my knickers, so I dropped it into the small stream directly beneath me.

After all the excitement and all the cash had been put safely away, Tom and Simon said, "Let's go and have some fun, Butlins here we come, and nobody tells anyone anythink, keep ya fat traps shut end off, no grassers in this gang."

I did not know what Butlins was or where it was, all I knew was that everyone was excited about getting to this place, little did I know that this place was going to be a place I visited a lot for the next year.

My feelings of excitement, elation and acceptance, that I was part of this great bunch of friends, friends that were my friends, that liked me enough to take me with them was fading very quickly. I was sticky and very hot and badly in need of a drink. I was beginning to feel very dizzy and strange, a feeling I had not come across before. I said out loud to the gang that I had to have a drink of water, and the older boys started laughing and in return said not long and we will be there, you can get all the drinks you want, look up, you can see Butlins. I looked up and could just make out some building in the distance, and with that everyone started walking faster to get there more quickly.

As we got closer and closer I could hear this rumbling noise, it sounded like thunder to me, then followed by this loud noise, there were people screaming. Simon then shouted out, "Oh I'm going on the Wild Mouse rollercoaster." Rollercoaster, I thought to myself, what is one of those, as we arrived at our destination. And there high up in the sky it was, the Wild Mouse, a long train of carriages with people and children inside them going very fast, up and down, then climbing very slowly up this steep piece of track, then doing a sharp turn, the carriage looking as if it was just about to topple over the edge and go crashing to the ground. At this point the people screamed the loudest, and I found it very frightening to watch, I was not going on that scary thing is what I said to myself in my head.

I followed the rest of the gang inside the building. It was darkish with lots of flashing lights, lots of people everywhere and the noise was deafening, sounds of machinery, metal scraping and banging, along with loud music mixed in with people chatting, laughing, screaming, and a beautiful aroma of food, popcorn and candy floss, all too much for my brain to be able to understand what all of this was.

At last we were all at the counter ordering drinks, candy floss and popcorn. I watched very closely to see what the others did and followed suit, and before long I had a large cup of orangeade in my hands. I took a large gulp of it to quickly quench my thirst and then I found I could no longer breath, my throat was stinging and felt that it had closed up, I was trying to swallow but the drink just wouldn't go down. Then I had a stinging sensation in my nose which caused my eyes to start watering, this was the very first time I had ever had a fizzy drink. If this is what fizzy drinks are like and it takes your breath away, then I don't want to have it again, I thought to myself.

All of my friends started laughing and said I will get used to it.

A plan of action was then put into place. If anyone got lost we would have a meeting point and the meeting point would be over there near the Ghost Train. The Ghost Train sounded terrifying to me, I thought there is definitely not going to be any chance of me getting lost, I was going to stick with them like glue.

I stood by and watched the older ones go on the rides; there were quite a lot of things I could not go on, being too young and too small, much to my dislike. I thought to myself at the time, I wish I was older and bigger then I could have gone on the things they were able to get onto. I was soon becoming bored, I had this money in my knickers and was not doing much with it, I had had enough and I wanted to go home.

When we all regrouped, I made it known that I wanted to go home as this Butlins place was boring. The older ones said, "Ok let's take the younger ones on the Ghost Train, after that we can all go into the Hall of Mirrors."

The Ghost Train looked very frightening! As we were standing in line to go on the ride, I could hear people screaming as they went inside and screaming with their hands held over their faces as they came out. My heart was pounding in sheer terror as I myself was ready to step into the ghost train, there was a strange strong pungent smell; it must have been the smell of ghosts.

The train started moving and I could hear the noise of the metal wheels making contact with the tracks. Just in front of me were these huge black double doors covered in cobwebs, a skeleton holding a scythe that would fall forward as you passed it to go through the creepy doors into the doom as if ready to chop you up and with a sudden spurt of cold ghost air blown in your face. As for the remainder of the ride and all the scary encounters held inside, I couldn't tell you as I kept my head down with my eyes permanently closed for the whole of the ride.

Never again would I put myself at the mercy of the Ghost Train.

I had no sense of time, it did not even occur to me that Mum and the rest of the family would be worrying about where I had got to, nor did I comprehend that I was in serious trouble when I did eventually turn up home under the sky of darkness.

It was decided that on our way home we would all grab a bag of chips and catch a bus back as it would have still been a long way to walk back and by this time it had been a very long day and all of us were very tired.

The bag of chips was freshly made and very hot with plenty of salt and vinegar, it was definitely soul soothing and certainly a big treat. It was very rare that you got a bag of chips in those days, and that only happened on special treat days which were few and far between.

It was dark, the street lights were on, I was still out and knew that I was in serious trouble when I made my home entrance. Walking into our street with the gang I found nerve-wracking; the street was empty and silent, the gang did not appear to be fazed that it was late, maybe their parents did not mind what their kids got up to or even mind how late they drifted back home. I said my "see ya" and parted company knocking on my own front door.

Mum opened the door and she was looking out over me to see who I had been with; the stern annoyed look Mum gave me told me straightaway I was in big trouble.

After much conversation, explaining to Mum where I had been and why I was so late did not change the punishment that I was going to receive.

I was grounded until further notice, not allowed to hang out or go anywhere with those police trouble kids, period. My sisters had to keep any eye on me, and if I tried to slip out they were instructed to report straight to Mum.

I found the grounding hard, I was miserable and back to square one, no friends. I started playing in the front garden in order to see my friends playing in the street. Susan came to the front garden gate to speak to me, she said, "Val, we are all going out tomorrow, if you want to come with us knock on early in the morning."

"I can't come out, Mum has grounded me, I'm not allowed to play with any of you anymore," I said.

"Come on Val, you won't be in any trouble, just sneak out."

"All right, I will try and get out, see you tomorrow."

I don't care what Mum does to me I thought to myself, they are my friends, and I am going no matter what.

I found it difficult to sleep that night, I was constantly worrying about what would happen to me when I disobeyed what Mum had said, but my friends were important, Mum just doesn't understand.

I slipped out early in the morning before any of my family stirred. I knocked on the door of my friends' house, their dogs started barking, and before I knew what was what, the dogs came screaming round to the front door barking and growling at me, showing their teeth getting ready to take a chunk out of my flesh. I was so terrified, these dogs were known for being highly vicious dogs and normally the back garden gate was always locked. Just as the black dog called Sam was about to try and sink his teeth into me Susan opened the door, "Quick get in," and with that Susan yanked me in just in the nick of time. I was saved by my friend otherwise there could have been a nasty situation.

I waited for everyone to get ready which was not long at all. I must have looked a state. Mum always did my hair, brushing it through and applying a hair cream called Vitapoint which made the hair soft and shiny, then put up in bunches or plaits finished off always with beautiful silk blue ribbons, giving off the look of a well looked after angelic little girl, who was now on her way to being a delinquent kid, out of control.

It was a beautiful hot summer's morning; we were all walking down the road heading towards the town centre. I felt great, what more could I ask for, I was with my friends and enjoying the summer rays pouring onto my skin and in a world of my own. I did not have a clue where we were going, and I did not care where we were going just as long as I was with my friends, life couldn't get any better.

We came across a bus stop which had wooden seating, and for some reason we all dived in and sat down. Simon and Tom started rolling some tobacco, just how I used to see my father do it and then all the blue smoke with a terrible putrid smell. Susan got given one and a box of matches and started lighting up the rolled cigarette, I was shocked; everyone was smoking except me.

Susan then said to me, "Come on Val, have a puff on this."

"I don't want to, I'm not allowed to smoke, only grownups are allowed to."

"It's alright, look this is how you do it, draw it back and quickly breathe it back real quick then blow it back out, simple, try it, watch me and do what I do, it's nice."

I watched closely and thought alright I will have one go.

I took hold of the rolled up cigarette, took a puff and blew it straight back out. "No, no you have to take it right back so it goes down the back of your throat."

"Oh right, ok like this," drawing it back and letting the smoke go right down into the back of my throat. The minute I did this I felt a burning sensation, a taste like I had swallowed a bonfire, I was then choking and coughing, I felt like I couldn't breathe and then all of a sudden I felt very dizzy.

At this point everyone was falling about laughing, I was told you will get used to it, I did get used to it and started to like it, my world was brilliant, I had friends, I was smoking, I was a grown up now.

We had been walking around for a long time going nowhere really just walking around aimlessly, I was tired, hungry and very thirsty, when both Simon and Tom said, "Let's go to the Unigate Milk yard, it will be empty now."

When we got there I could see all the milk floats parked up and plugged into the electric where the floats were being charged up for the early morning round of delivering the milk. I had noticed another strong pungent smell of sour milk; it was everywhere in the air.

At the back of the milk floats they all had little glass cabin cupboards and you could see items of food inside them, butter and dairy products and above these was a silver looking cupboard and these were locked. So we went round and tried every single one and then a few were not locked. They contained biscuits, bread and other items; these were taken out and eaten straight away.

All of us were desperate for a drink but everything else was locked up with massive padlocks on them, then someone shouted "Let's get the milk machine in front of the building," and with that, Simon and Tom were gone.

By the time Susan and I got there the milk machine had already been ripped open with full access to the cartons of milk which were in the shape of triangles in this kind of wax cover containing the milk, with Unigate milk plastered all over it. By now everyone seemed to be in some kind of frenzy ripping out the cartons of milk drinking them and also using the milk that had not been consumed smashing it as hard as they could to make milk bombs which exploded on the ground and also the walls. By the time this had all been done, it really was such an ugly sight with empty exploded milk cartons and milk spewed everywhere, then the classic call that I would hear over and over again, "Fucking leg it."

We all ended up smack bang in the middle of the town centre and were passing a green grocers shop which had a side gate to the back of the shop. Before I knew what was happening, everyone was climbing over this gate. I soon followed suit and ended up walking along this very high brick wall which took us behind all of the shops on that side of the town centre. In the back of the green grocers was a very strong stench of rotting cabbages and carrots with thousands of small flies engulfing that area. I couldn't wait to get past this shop as I was not very good with funny smells making me feel sick.

The others seem to walk quite quickly high above the ground, where I was terrified that I was going to fall off and receive some serious injuries.

The gang was out of sight, I was on this high brick wall on my own, I started crying, I couldn't get down, there was nowhere else to go except forward, arms out each side as if I was walking the tight rope to keep my balance. The more I thought about where I actually was and what I was doing, the harder it became for me to keep my balance and not go crashing off the wall into the unknown.

Susan came back as she could hear me crying, "What's wrong Val, why are you crying? Come on give me your hand." And with that and placing my hand in Susan's hand, I felt safe, I was not going to tumble off the wall.

The wall then turned a corner and came to a dead end; there was no sight of the others. Susan then said to me to follow her, and I noticed that a window was open and with a little jump, Susan had leapt to the window and was now scrambling up through the window with just her feet in sight, and then she was gone. I was expected to do the same.

I then took my leap to the window, it wasn't open after all, the window had been smashed and glass was everywhere. I tried with all my might to pull myself up and over the glass to get in, I called for Susan to come and help me, she came straightaway and told me to shut up and be quiet and to use my feet against the wall to help lever myself up and over the glass to get in. I tried and this worked, but as I was coming through, my dress got caught on some glass and it ripped as I clumsily made it through the window. I knew straightaway that I would be in deep trouble with Mum, let alone that I had disobeyed her order not to come out with these kids.

Once inside I noticed that we were inside the Co-op store. I found this quite exciting being inside this shop in the dark and with no customers, I still did not grasp that what we were doing was wrong or even that it was a criminal activity.

The older lads had got a bag and were stuffing loads of watches and other things into it. I myself went to the

102

till pressing the buttons as if I was playing shops, nothing entering my head that what had taken place or myself being in this shop was wrong in anyway. I liked playing these games and the adrenaline rush that accompanied the signal, "Fucking leg it," that echoed through as if in slow motion.

The alarm bells started ringing, everyone had scrambled through the windows leaving me behind in a disarrayed shop; it looked like a bomb had gone off. I found it hard to jump up and get to the smashed window, panic and fear entered in only for the reason that I was in the shop totally alone.

Eventually I grabbed up at the smashed window with my left hand receiving sudden severe pain. With no time to lose, I pulled myself up through the window, I was out with no fear of the high brick wall, I was running as fast as I could to catch up with my friends who were nowhere to be seen.

Eventually I came to the entrance of the green grocers, thank God, and to my relief I now knew that I only had to climb over the gate and I would be back in the town centre. It was quite dark now with the street lamps shining, but still no sight of the others. I had to make my own way back home, blood was pouring from my hand which had swollen up. I could feel something sharp at the entrance of the wound; it was a piece of glass. I bravely pulled as much of the glass out as possible, then started to wipe my hand on my dress; to this day I still have the scar on my hand and when I press it I feel pain as I still believe I have some fragments of glass in the scar tissue.

I arrived in my street with not a soul about, I couldn't even say what the time was, but it certainly was no time for a 7-year-old child to be out, let alone walking back from the town centre, that must have been 2 miles.

I was starting to feel fearful and I knew I was in big trouble with Mum for disobeying her. For some reason I thought if I went round to the back of the house and knocked on the back door, I would be in less trouble. The full moon was out and this created much more light to see where I was going. I took a big gulp and knocked on the door and within seconds Mum opened the door, her hand grabbed me and with that I was yanked inside.

Mum was very angry and told me she had been worried out of her mind with me being gone all day, not knowing where I was and if I was safe or not. Questions were being fired at me and I remembered what the gang had told me; never grass, no grassers in this gang, so I made up some story that I was at a massive park that was a long way away, I got lost and couldn't find my way back home. I was now lying to my mum, she already knew that I was lying to her because she had gone over to the gangs' house and had been told that I took off with the rest of the kids early in the morning. Mum told me she already knew who I was with. I received a good hiding from Mum, the first time ever, I felt really bad lying to Mum.

Over the next few days I stayed home, I did not like being stuck indoors with no chance of being able to go outside, even the garden was off limits to me.

I was upstairs looking out of the front bedroom window, when I saw police cars outside the gangs' house, but it still did not dawn on me that I had been involved in some kind of criminal activity. I thought why are the police at the gangs' house? All I knew was that I wanted to go and knock on for them.

More days had passed, I was becoming more restless and feeling resentful towards Mum and my sisters, who were all happy playing inside the house and also the garden.

A knock at the front door, I rushed to open it, Susan asked if I was coming out to play.

"I can't, my mum has told me I am not allowed to go out anywhere with anyone."

"You can sneak out without her seeing you, we are all going out this afternoon."

"I can't, I was in big trouble before, I got a good hiding as well, I don't want another one."

"Oh come on Val, I will speak to her when we get back, so you don't get in trouble."

"Alright then, I will come out, just as long as you speak to my mum so I don't get in any trouble with her."

I might have been forward in a lot of things, but in my 7-year-old mind, I really did think that if my friend Susan spoke to Mum, I wouldn't be in any trouble whatsoever for disobeying her again.

Susan told me to keep my eyes open for them; they will wait for me just outside the fence at the front of my house.

I remember exactly what I was wearing that very day, it was a cotton dress that Mum had made for me, the colours on it were a deep yellow base colour with deep orange floral prints of swirls that were quite harmful to the eyes to look at, but was the in thing all those years ago. It was cheap and cheerful. Mum at the time was on her own with 4 young kids, debt was building up and life was getting harder and harder, Mum was sinking deeper and deeper into depression, and finding it harder to put food on the table.

I remember seeing Mum crying a lot, I did not know the reason why, even if Mum told me I would not really have any understanding of any of it.

I was having severe pain in my stomach the same feeling I had when we were living at the bungalow, hunger pains. Mum had no money until she was able to draw her income support on Monday morning, the cupboards were bare.

I said to Mum, "My tummy is hurting, I'm really hungry."

"I know Val; your sisters are hungry too. I've run out of food, I will make some bread rolls, it won't be long, just try and hold on a little longer."

The pains in my stomach started to become more and more intense, I had a burning sensation followed by severe cramp style pain where I would bend over holding onto my stomach in order to obtain some kind of ease, but every time I tried to put myself in an upright position, the pain just got worse it felt like a thousand knives jabbing me inside.

I could now smell and taste the full aromas wafting through the house of fresh bread; this made my situation worse than before, I started whimpering then I went into full blown crying mode as before, the more I cried the better I would feel, the pains easing away with crying.

I could now stand upright. I made my way to the kitchen as Mum was just removing the bread rolls from the oven, "When can we have some bread Mum? I can't wait any longer."

"You have to wait until they have cooled down, not long now."

I had noticed that the gang was waiting outside the front of the house near the fence, I no longer cared about being hungry, my excitement about going out with the gang had priority above all else. I slipped out the front door and was gone, not knowing what adventure lay ahead.

Once out of the street Susan sparked up a fag, "Here you go Val, have a puff of this." I couldn't wait to try it again and definitely did not want to be the odd one out.

I had noticed that Tom had something in his hands that I had never seen before, it was a metal object that had once been painted red, but the paint had worn off. Later on in my life I had learnt that it was a half size crowbar, and unbeknown to me, the lads were fully equipped for a pre-meditated robbery, everyone else knew except me.

It was late Sunday afternoon and the sky held a beautiful red glow to it with a gentle warm feeling in the air, red sky at night shepherd's delight always came to mind.

We arrived at the Marina, it was low tide, you could see all the green seaweed and smell the strong pungent smell that accompanied the marina, seaweed mixed up with the petrol oily smell with the black mushy silt mud that lay at the side of the marina when the tide was low, the boats sitting there still and lifeless for a late Sunday afternoon.

The area had lots of boating yards; the little ones all fenced off with fishing boats lay derelict, the old paint all worn off, where the actual wood was disintegrating from lack of use and no longer needed. Old fishing nets with old cork floats that once proudly held the nets afloat to harbour the fish that entered the nets of doom, yet still giving of an aroma of fish.

We all ended up at the biggest boating yard of all, it was close to the harbours' edge with a small narrow road that separated it from the ocean. The front gates were the biggest I had ever seen, holding a chain and huge padlock, and I could see contained within the confines of this boating yard, beautiful luxurious yachts held up high in the air nestled upon giant scaffolding whilst they were being repaired, painted or whatever else needed to be done.

Walking around the perimeter of the fence, the lads suddenly said, "all in here quickly before we are seen." We entered at the side of the fence which was enclosed with bramble like wild bushes and this ended up being quite a painful passage, past these things grabbing and scratching you like unwinding triffids, arms stretched out trying to tangle you in.

We were all standing at the side of the main office building of this boating yard, and there high up showed a small window, which could be reached once you climbed up the fence with a concrete post that could be balanced upon within easy reach of the window.

Tom was up and at the window asking someone to pass him the crowbar, yet still to me, I did not have any knowledge or realise that anything unlawful was happening; I was too young to even have that kind of thinking, of any responsibility. All I can remember at the time was the feeling of being excited and most of all the wonderful words of, "Fucking leg it," which meant to me run as fast as you could with shaky legs and a pumping heart.

We all stood there looking up in silence as Tom prized open the window with the crowbar and was in the building with a blink of an eye, Simon was up and in as quick as a flash.

It seemed a long time waiting to me and I just wanted to go home and get something to eat as the hunger pains were back again; it was boring just standing there waiting, waiting for what I did not know.

Soon enough an off-white cream material bag was thrown out of the window and landed in front of us with a big thud as it hit the ground. Susan grabbed the bag and it was very heavy, she undid the knot and there before my eyes I could see, it was stuffed with coins... money. Then another bag came flying through the window, Susan undid the knot and there inside were loads of bank notes all rolled up in bundles. She put it alongside the other bag, then another bag dropped before us and contained the same rolled up bank notes.

I looked up and Simon was making an exit out of the window, but he remained on the fence as Tom made his way out holding a big black tin which he passed to Simon to grab hold of. With that Simon asked Susan to reach up and grab the tin he was passing to her, and in a fumbling fashion, Susan grabbed the black tin box which then slipped out of her hands and landed on the ground where I was standing. The box had some considerable weight behind it as I tried to move it.

Once altogether on ground level, the lads were very excited and squealing quietly, laughing and saying, "We've hit the fucking jackpot."

The bag of coins was far too heavy to carry, so Susan started stuffing coins into her pockets. Once again I had no pockets just a cotton summer dress on, so I picked up the bottom of my dress to form a pocket and I started stuffing the coins into my dress then grabbing the end to have some kind of knot to the hold the coins.

All of a sudden bells started ringing, it was the alarm bell, and once again the words were hollered out, "Fucking leg it, train station." I ran as fast as I could, trying to keep up with the rest of them, and as I was running, a lot of the coins I had were spilling out everywhere, but I just kept going.

As we had become a safe distance away from the boating yard with all of us heading for the train station, the lads told everyone to slow down so as to not draw any attention to ourselves; we had to get under the crawl space of the train station without anyone seeing us. I remember that I was so excited about going under and into the crawl space under the train station above all else. Surprisingly it was not dark at all, not how I would have imagined it to be, for some reason I thought it would be a dark place, but all the lighting from the train station above kept the underneath crawl space just as well lit.

When we were all under the safety of the crawl space, Tom prized open the black tin with the crowbar to reveal more bank notes inside.

"Right," Tom said, "everyone put all the money here on the ground," and with those instructions the money was put where he had stated, but I only had loose change and not much left at that either as I had dropped a lot of it when I was running.

Everyone then started unrolling the notes which were being placed into the black tin box; there were loads and loads of bank notes so many, that the black tin could not be closed.

The rest of the bank notes were now being dished out and shared equally, the wad of notes I had was so great that I couldn't even hold it in my hands. So I took a bunch of twenty pound notes and placed them inside my shoes which made my shoes feel very tight when I put my shoes back on. I also placed some notes into my knickers, and everyone else put the bank notes everywhere they could be placed, pockets, knickers, shoes, socks.

It was then agreed that no one would come here on their own, everyone would come back together to get more cash when we needed it.

Simon then proceeded to start digging a hole in the ground with the crowbar to hide the tin and when that was all done and the tin safely hidden, a stick was poked in the spot so we would know exactly where it was hidden.

It was then agreed and the code of honour within the gang reaffirmed, tell no one, no grassers in this gang and with a quick shake of the hands, it was time to head back home.

Just before I was ready to knock on the back door, I had found a little shrub directly under the kitchen window of my home. Quickly I removed all the wad of notes from my shoes and knickers and hid the money tucked away right behind the bush.

My God was I in serious trouble! I received the hiding of my life from Mum and from then on my life was totally kept under the watchful eye of my mother, I had to be glued to her at all times, I was never ever going to get the chance of absconding ever again.

I found a plastic see-through bag and thought this would be great to put the wad of notes in just for safety, as our toilet was on the outside of the house. I managed to get outside quickly to the bush and get the notes inside the bag and put it all back again hidden and safe.

Looking outside the front bedroom window over to the gangs' house, there was no sighting of the gang at all.

Two weeks had passed by and still no sighting of my friends and by this time, Mum was starting to relax a bit and I no longer had to be permanently in her sight.

Then all of a sudden, I got sight of my friends who were now hanging out in front of my front garden fence.

I went straightaway to Mum and asked her if could just stand in the front garden and talk to my friend Susan, I promised that I would not go further than the front gate, and with a lot of begging and pleading Mum gave in but told me she would be watching me fully from the window.

Susan told me that everyone was laying low and that her mum and dad know about the money, but do not know about the rest of the money hidden under the railway station. They too had been in serious trouble and also grounded, and their mum had taken the money off them and used it to pay off bills and buy food and clothes.

Susan then said that it was all in the newspapers about the robbery and the police had said that the robbery had been done by some highly professional robbers who as yet had not been found, but investigations were still ongoing. The robbery was a significant haul, and if any member of public has seen anything suspicious around the time, please contact the CID immediately.

This information meant nothing to me as I still did not know that I had been involved in any wrongdoing, Susan might as well have been talking to me in another language. It did not dawn on me until much later on in my adult life when the alarm bells started ringing, the magnitude of what I had been involved in.

There was only one more week to go before the school summer holidays were over, and in that last week Mum had set me free to go and play outside but only in the front of the house in the street, or in the back on the field so that she could have a full view of me at all times.

One day I managed to slip off with the gang. I grabbed some notes from the bag, put some twenty pound notes in my shoes and off I went.

The gang said that we were off to the beach and the Marina to go on the speed boats. I had seen the speed boats in action and had always wanted to go on one, but at the time my Grandmother took us to the beach, she always said no, it was too expensive. It was the best time in my life, we had many goes on the boat, and I remember with all the loose change I was told to throw it into the sea for good luck. The boat was going at high speed jumping up and down and crashing hard on the waves, my hair being pushed hard backwards and with lots of sea spray in my face every time the boat came crashing back down.

I had never laughed so much, it was exhilarating, the feelings and emotions I had from that day remained with me for the rest of my life.

I arrived home at a normal time and before tea. Mum had asked me where I had been as she could not see me in the fields. I was becoming quite a liar, I actually did not like lying to Mum, I did know that was very wrong and did not like myself much for doing so, but I had to stick to the code of honour – no grassers in this gang. I told my mum I was over the Rec playing in the sandpit, I knew very well that on that part of the Rec you cannot be seen, and Mum accepted that as my answer. That was close I thought to myself.

The next day I slipped a twenty pound note in each shoe, I didn't have any socks on as it was still very hot coming to the end of the summer holidays. I got away again, this time we were going to the pictures. By the time we had walked the two miles to the town centre, I had to retrieve a twenty pound note from my shoe, and I was shocked at what I discovered; the ink from the note had started to rub off, was it useable? I did not know but the lady at the kiosk accepted it anyway, but what intrigues me now, is why not one person ever questioned what a little kiddy was doing with a large amount of money.

I had still had the other twenty pound note in my other shoe, and I also had change in the form of a five pound note after attending the pictures, I was not going to put this into my shoe incase the same thing happened again with the ink rubbing off, but yet I still left the other note still in my shoe.

I arrived home and Mum did not detect a thing. I hurried to my stash that was hidden to put the money back inside the bag, and just as I finished Mum was standing there right behind me.

The first words Mum said to me were, "Val, why do you keep coming to this bush? What have you got in there?" I could not say a word, I was scared and couldn't think of anything quick enough to tell Mum. With that I was moved out of the way so Mum could investigate what was so special about this bush. Mum pulled out the plastic bag and put her hand to her mouth in shock at what she had found, I was grabbed by the arm and hurried indoors.

Mum was horrified, "Where in the hell did you get all this money Valerie? Don't lie to me, I want the truth, where has it come from?"

I blurted out, "I found it in the street ages ago Mum, I'm not lying, that is the truth, you can have it Mum, I don't want it."

"Is that the truth Val? Because if I find out you have been lying to me, you will get the biggest hiding you have ever had in your life young lady."

I never heard any more about it, although Mum said one day, "What would you really like to have from that money you found?"

To which I answered, "I would like to have a record player that I can play records on and sing to."

I had a love of music and just loved singing along to Diana Ross and the Supremes. My record player was my pride and joy and gave me a lot of happiness and was something I could escape into later on in life.

My life beginning at an early recording.

A quick click of the camera, the momentous occasion captured forever.

Our little mixed raced family, me sucking my thumb far right.

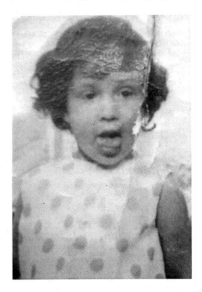

Me with my lightweight cotton dress with big orange spots.

My Nan and mum with my sisters.

My angel sister Hazel, far right, age 5.

Me and Nan at the beach.

Me and my sister Paula, outside our pre-fabricated bungalow
for homeless families.

My sister Hazel, having her photo in our overgrown derelict garden.

Me with my offensive dress age 8, with mum and my brother Ivan.

My youngest sister Paula, delighted with her new doll.

The entrance to get to school, hasn't changed much from this old Victorian photo.

The cut through I had to use, today, remains unchanged.

The huge gravestone I passed everyday age 4, absolutely
terrifying.

Me and my mum today, closer than ever and stronger with plenty of confidence.

My beautiful mum and sister Paula.

My mum age 17.

I was catapulted into a different world, a new dimension.
I took a big deep breath, and headed forward.

Chapter 5

Arrested and in Police Hands

9.12.1970 Interviewed by C.I.D. Littlehampton, concerning thefts during mid-term holidays, I was 8 years old. In total there was a list of 56 offences. I as an 8-year-old child had no comprehension that I had done anything wrong. In the police interview it was recorded that I had admitted to every single one, a child in the hands of the police, arrested and finger printed without Mum, I was on my own.

I was treated as an offender aged 18 years old the only difference being, 10 years was missing from my age.

I was fascinated at having my finger prints taken even though I did not know why or even what it meant having this procedure done; to me it was having all your fingers covered in black ink and making marks on paper, something any child would enjoy, playing around with paint and inks to make your handprint. The policeman took hold of each of my fingers and then in one continuous motion rolled each finger onto the paper. I liked the look of all my fingers transferred onto paper, I thought it looked pretty. I did ask the policeman if I could take it home, his answer was simply, "NO."

I was shown where the sink was with soap to wash my hands and given paper towels to dry them, but as hard as I tried, the ink just would not come off. There was also a sticky feel to my fingers, and by this time I was starting to get very upset because to me my hands were dirty.

After the police interview by the C.I.D., without the presence of Mum, the police took me home in a police car and just dropped me off, they did not see or even speak to Mum.

I went into the house and did not say anything about where I had been, I just sat down and duly had my tea. I have no idea why I did not let Mum know that I had been in the police station, the only thing that springs to mind is that I must have thought it was too unimportant to say anything.

LIST OF OFFENCES ADMITTED BY VALERIE LAWSON.

LIST OF OFFENCES ADMITTED BY VALERIE LAWSON

1. Between 1st and 12th May, 1970 — Entered house through open window and stole theatrical costumes

2. Between 23rd and 30th March, 1970 — Stole apples from shop display

3. Saturday, 2nd May, 1970 — Entered St. Mary's Church, stole sweets from pocket of coat left on cycle

4. Sunday, 3rd May, 1970 — Stole 1s 7d. from purse left with clothing on beach

5. Sunday, 10th May, 1970 — Stole sweets from counter of shop

6. Friday, 24th May, 1970 — Stole tin containing cash from newsvendor's stand

7. Between 1st and 30th September, 1970 — Entered car through insecure door and stole plastic bag containing pennies

8. Between 18th and 19th April, 1970 — Climbed on to cinema roof, gaining access to yard at rear of shop, stole carrots

9. Saturday, 25th April, 1970 — Went to insecure car parked in grounds of private school and stole purse containing cash, and torch

10. Between 1st and 31st January, 1970 — Went to insecure car on waste land. Removed cash from purse, replaced purse in shopping bag

11. Between 1st and 14th September, 1970 — Stole candy floss from confectioner's stall in amusement park

12. Sunday, 26th April, 1970 — Went to vehicle parked in grounds of private school, inserted hand through open window, stole purse and cash

13. Between 1st and 20th December, 1969 — Stole 1 lb. apples from rear of shop

14. Between 1st and 9th May, 1970 — Went to insecure vehicle in school grounds, stole sweets from shopping bag on driving seat

15. Between 1st and 31st March, 1970 — Picked bunch of flowers from front garden of house

16. Between 1st and 31st January, 1970 — Went to unlocked car in cinema car park, stole washing-up liquid which was then squeezed over the windscreens of other vehicles

17. Between 12th and 30th April, 1970 — Went to unlocked vehicle in car park. Removed loose cash from pocket of man's coat which was hanging in vehicle

18. Saturday, 9th May, 1970 — Stole holdall from windbreak on beach

19	Between 1st and 31st March, 1970	Whilst owner was painting beach hut, removed sunglasses from bag on beach in front of beach hut
20	21st July, 1970	Burglary at 82 Parkside Avenue, L'ton by breaking into sun lounge at rear, and a garden shed. Stole 2 dolls and a lighter (shown)
21	Between 15th and 16th May, 1970	Broke window in door at rear of milk float, stole biscuits
22	27th July, 1970	Entered Gamley's shop and stole purses from display
23	1st August, 1970	Went to hut on beach used as store, stole purse and cash
24	5th August, 1970	Entered fisherman's hut and stole rods and reels
25	5th August, 1970	Entered shed at side of river by smashing pane of glass and climbing through, stole binoculars
26	5th August, 1970	Forced down partially open window of vehicle, stole cash and cheque books
27	2nd August, 1970	Stole bunch of keys from Amusement Arcade
28	5th August, 1970	Took stick of rock from shop display
29	5th August, 1970	Stole property from rear of unattended milk float at dairy
30	5th August, 1970	Stole cigarette and matches from unattended lorry
31	5th August, 1970	Stole chocolate from display in café
32	5th August, 1970	Stole cigarettes and matches from cabin of sailing boat at West Beach
33	2nd August, 1970	Stole cash from church offertory box, St.Mary's Church, Littlehampton
34	5th August, 1970	Smashed window of unoccupied house, were about to enter but were disturbed and ran off
35	4th August, 1970	Smashed pane of glass in window at rear of Littlehampton Youth Club, climbed through and stole sweets and squash
36	Between 24th and 31st July, 1970	Opened closed but unlocked window at Maud Allan School, entered premises and stole keys
37	2nd August, 1970	Smashed pane of glass in Croquet Club on Sports Field, entered and stole biscuits.

Between 27th and 28th July, 1970	Went to Dairy, forced locker on unattended milk float and stole food and drink
Sunday, 19th July, 1970	Entered workshop in grounds of private school by unlocked door, searched through suitcases belonging to pupils. Were disturbed and detained by loser
Saturday, 18th July, 1970	Stole knife from tent on beach
(Came home) Between 31st October & 2nd November, 1970	Entered Littlehampton Museum by removing plastic ventilator from rear window, inserting hand and opening catch, then climbing through. Stole a number of ancient coins
Between 1st and 31st August, 1970	Removed purse from pocket of coat hanging in changing room at Sports Field
Between 15th and 16th August, 1971	Attempted to enter Angmering Working Men's Club by smashing window
15th August, 1971	Entered Methodist Church and Hall, L'ton, by forcing rear window and climbing through. Stole small amount of cash (No money taken)
(numbered day before) Between 2nd and 3rd June, 1971	Entered lock-up shoe shop by smashing pane of glass at rear, removing glass and climbing through. Stole footwear
Between 30th and 31st July, 1971	Entered St.Wilfred's School, Angmering, by means of open window-nothing stolen
Between 30th and 31st July, 1971	Entered St.Margaret's School,Angmering, by open window, damaged property inside
Between 14th and ... August, 1971	Entered builder's workshop by removing pane of glass from window and climbing through. Stole a screwdriver
Between 15th and 16th August, 1971	Entered St.Wilfred's School, Angmering, by removing part of plastic ventilator, inserting hand, releasing catch and climbing through. Nothing stolen
Between October and December, 1970	Stole fruit from store at rear of greengrocer's shop
Sunday, 15th August, 1971	Entered St.Mary's Church Hall, L'ton, through insecure window and consumed biscuits and drink on premises
Between 30th and 31st July, 1971	Entered parked and unattended motor car by slitting canvas roof. Stole pair of sunglasses from glove compartment
31st October, 1971	Entered St.Catherine's Catholic Church, L'ton, stole offertory box and rosaries.

16.

(19 admissions)
(14 admissions.)

County of West Sussex

PETTY SESSIONAL DIVISION OF ARUNDEL

John A. Henham, Solicitor
Clerk to the Justices

Tel: Litt. 4106   My ref: ET      Your ref: R/G

JUSTICES' CLERK'S OFFICE,
COUNTY BUILDINGS,
EAST STREET,
LITTLEHAMPTON.

24th December, 1971

Dear Sirs,

Police -v- Mrs. Nancy Lawson - Valerie Maria Lawson

I refer to your letter of 23rd December, 1971 and write to inform you that the hearing arranged for the Special Juvenile Court on the 31st December, 1971 in respect of the above matter has been adjourned to Friday, 14th January, 1972 at 10.30 a.m. at The Council Chamber, Littlehampton.

I trust you will inform Mrs. Lawson as she has been summoned to attend on 31st December, 1971.

Yours faithfully,

Clerk to the Justices.

Messrs. C. F. Snow & Co.,
Solicitors,
16/18, Beach Road, Littlehampton.

Copy to E. Beatty Esq.,
Principal Area Social Worker,
Littlehampton Area Office,
2, Linden Chambers, Bognor Regis, Sussex.

Superintendent of Police, Littlehampton, Sussex

14.8.1970 I was taken to a children's home. I really did not want to leave home but under the circumstances it was in my best interests; I had gone off the rails and was hanging out with children a lot older than me with a big tendency to the life of crime. I still had no idea that crimes were and had been committed by these children, all that mattered to me was that I had friends who did not ever call me horrible names, that I was at long last accepted.

I was out of control, rude, cheeky and most of all it did not matter how much Mum tried to control me, I still went off with the older children regardless.

With agreement between the children's social services and Mum, I had to go into a reception centre so everyone could have some breathing space and start to concentrate on the 56 offences that had been attributed to me by the police.

A Reception Report had been written about me and reads:-

"Valerie had not been able to talk to any extent about why she'd had to leave home although at the time, she had been able to talk a little about her need to leave home because of the damage it was doing to her; she was uncontrollable as long as the older children were there.

She was quite strange about her clothing, not only did she refuse to change for P.E. at school but in the centre she was always extremely reluctant to bath and preferred to wash with all her clothes on and her nightie on top. She would take off her trousers and sweater, put on her nightie or pajamas and her dressing-gown on top and then get into bed with the lot on; she seemed very young to be showing such modesty at this stage and it was more likely that it was a question of her colour. She might feel that she could get away with it from the neck upwards but that it became more obvious when she was undressed. She had been helped by having her long curly hair cut into a short and very attractive style which was far more manageable and made her more like the other girls.

Valerie

Valerie is 8 years of age, coloured, and the eldest of four girls.

She was admitted on 14.08.70 during the school holidays.

Although upset at her removal from home, she settled into residential care quite easily, helped by the fact that mother visited soon after her admission and at regular intervals after that.

She is a rather odd little girl who can mix quite adequately within her own age group and yet remains at one remove in the group situation, she is always in the group and yet never quite part of it, she has no close friend.

In relationships with adults she feels more comfortable with females.

She is amenable and fairly easy to control. Initially she needed correction and walked away muttering curses but now she is more accepting of correction and reacts in a more normal way."

At the children's home, Reception Centre I was absolutely amazed at the sheer size of the building, and to me it was the most beautiful building inside and out. It was all Tudor, the massive double arched oak doors with all the thick black metal fixings along with black metal knots, you would have expected Henry VIII to come walking out of these doors.

All the windows were of Tudor style with leaded lights. Once through the main entrance doors you were then led to the full glory of a massive Tudor grand staircase that held the most beautiful deep red carpet with gold metal carpet holders holding the carpet in the correct position and then white paint at the sides. It took my breath away; as I had said before I was always fascinated by history and old buildings, I could not wait to explore.

I was feeling very upset on the day I was being taken away from my home; all I knew was that I had been so naughty that I was being put into a children's home for punishment. My social worker who was male put me in his car and that was it. I did not say a word on the journey, I could not physically say one word as I was so terrified going into the unknown, being with people I did not know and most of all, I had not been told how long I would have to stay there. I could feel a lump building up in my throat and a great sadness washing over me, I would no longer see my sisters or my mum, once again I was on my own. I could not comprehend any of it, I shut down and stayed shut down for my duration in the children's home. On the outside no one would get through, but on the inside I was very much alive and absorbing all the beauty that surrounded me.

We had arrived and drove up a gravel driveway which produced in front of my eyes this remarkable Tudor building.

I did not have a suitcase; my clothing was so sparse that it was just popped into a carrier bag,

My worldly goods consisted of:

1 Tan trousers and waistcoat
1 Peach cardigan
1 Red cardigan
1 Pink nylon petticoat
1 Pair pink pajamas
3 Cotton summer dresses
3 Pairs white socks (2 white and 1 pink)
1 Vest
2 Pairs pants (1 pink 1 white)
1 Red coat
1 Pair red sandals
1 Pair navy pants

Not very much for an 8-year-old child by any stretch of the imagination!

My social worker took me inside and told me to sit down and wait until he came back. I could hear the muffled sound of children going about their business which caused me to feel very alarmed and frightened of what these children would have in store for me. Was I going to get beaten up, called Nigger or Wog or Blacky?

The very thought made my stomach do a complete somersault.

I could see my social worker with a lady heading towards me, he duly gave me her name and then said to me that he would come back soon to see how I had settled in and with that he was gone.

This lady did not seem very nice at all, she had a very stern and stone like face, and never did she produce a smile and only said to me, "Come with me."

This lady took me upstairs via the grand staircase, I was enjoying this experience very much, taking in all the splendor and noticing the most beautiful dark oak shiny handrail. In between each side of the stairs it was white stone like porcelain pillars, very much like you would see in Roman Greek buildings, I had to touch it to see what it felt like, it was cold to the touch.

Reaching the top of the staircase before me was the biggest landing I had ever seen with the deep red velvet carpet covering everywhere. The walls were all covered in deep oak panels, the ceiling which was very high was adorned with large oak beams, then hanging from the ceiling were two large crystal chandeliers; it was breathtaking. This lady taking me upstairs would never in her wildest dreams have ever imagined an 8-year-old child having these thought processes.

Tucked away in the corner there were modern pink lockers with pigeonholes to gain entry and to the far left I could see a locker with my name on it. These lockers had been redesigned, where doors had been made with a circular hole for a finger to be inserted to open the door, this was referred to as pigeon hole lockers, but no pigeons ever nested in them.

"Right," she said, "this is your locker and all your personal items will be kept in here. Take your clothes out of your bag and put it in your locker, I will then take you to your dorm which is the pink bedroom and show you where your bed will be."

I never uttered a word, just listened to her instructions and duly did what she commanded.

There were 4 dorms, the pink dorm that consisted of 8 beds, and the yellow, green and brown dorms. I was told that this area was the girls' area, and across the landing on the other side was the boys' dorm and under no circumstances, were the girls allowed in the boys' area.

I was shown where my bed was in the dorm and was told that the side cabinet was mine to use and that paper and envelopes were provided and kept in the top draw, but that postage would have to be paid by myself.

Postage I thought to myself, what is postage; I really did not know what she meant.

The lady then instructed me to follow her again, and we stopped at these white cupboards which had a padlock on them. With a swish of her keys the door was opened and thrown into my hands were a toothbrush, Gibbs toothpaste, towel, soap and a small bottle of shampoo.

I was then informed that these items had to last me one week before I would be re-issued again with the same items.

The lady again instructed me to follow her and I was led to this big room adorned with a row of sinks with mirrors on the left side of me, forward in front of me were toilet cubicles' and to the right of me were a collection of baths with little blue chairs by each bath. She then duly told me, "This is where you come each morning to have your wash, brush your teeth, and over there is where you have a bath in the evenings, and in front of you are the toilets, now follow me to the bath area."

This lady was not very nice or very welcoming either to an 8-year-old child who has just been removed from her family who was also terrified about what was going to be expected of her.

"My name is Mrs Howard, I am now going to run a bath for you, go over there and take all your clothes off, and sit on the stool."

Whilst saying all that the bath water was running, "Wait a few seconds whilst I go and get you some clothes."

I sat there, feeling scared and did not want to take all my clothes off, I did not know this lady and I certainly did not want my clothes off in front of a complete stranger, so I just sat there frozen to the spot unable to move an inch.

Mrs Howard came marching in clutching some items and a cream plastic bag, she looked at me with very stern eyes. She put the items she was carrying on the floor and started seeing to the bath water, now mixing in the cold water, when she was done the taps were turned off.

Mrs Howard then turned her focus on me and said, "You were instructed to remove all your clothing as you need to have a bath, come on hurry up and get it all off."

I then said to this scary lady, "My mum has already given me a bath before I came here, so I don't need another."

"I don't care how many baths you have had prior to coming here, I have told you that you are having a bath here, now do what you are being told and get those clothes off now young lady!"

I still would not remove my clothes. Mrs Howard then reached out towards me trying to start the process of removing my clothes for me, but I pushed her hand away, this was the worst move I ever made, this made her very angry and then she was shouting at me reducing me to tears.

Mrs. Howard said to me, "You are a very naughty, rude and insolent girl, you will be doing exactly what you are told to do here, if you don't take off your clothes this instant, then you will be taken to the wardens' office straight away."

I took my clothes off, then the clothes were put into this plastic bag, there was me sitting there completely naked, I was trying to hide my bits, I felt absolutely humiliated, very scared and unsure of the situation, the most strange feelings came over me.

After what seemed like ages, Mrs Howard was still just standing there staring and looking at me so I began to feel unsafe, why is she not helping me into the bath, I thought to myself, I said to her, "Can I have a towel to cover myself, I don't like how you are looking at me."

Mrs Howard then said, "You don't have anything I have not got, get in that bath you horrible girl."

That was my welcome to the Reception Centre which was going to be my place of residence for an unknown period.

I went to the pink dorm and sat on my allocated bed, my hair was dripping wet. I did not really know how to sort my hair out, it was very long and I was used to Mum drying it, brushing it and putting Vitapoint cream into it, then tying into bunches or plaits with beautiful blue ribbon.

Eventually my hair dried on its own and it was frizzy; it looked like I was some wild unkempt child who was the exact replica of the wild man of Borneo. I did not know how bad I really looked, but it was noted in the Reception Centre observation report that they had to cut my hair short to make me fit in and look like the other girls.

I remember trying to put a brush through my hair, but the hair brush could not go through it as my hair was a mass of knots looking like an unruly bird's nest. I was becoming very upset and stressed that I could not brush my hair.

It did not take me very long to familiarise myself with the whole complex and I got to know every square inch. I was always interested in exploring my surroundings in order to find places to hide just in case the need arose, a place of safety.

I started to move around unnoticed and decided to go into the TV room, this was the room that the older girls would hang out in watching television, chatting, laughing and enjoying themselves. I will never ever forget my first time in the TV room, Top of the Pops was on playing the current No 1 at the time, Band of Gold by Freda Payne. I slipped in quietly and sat at the back close to the double bay window enjoying the music. I truly loved the song and would be singing to it in my mind, I loved the vocals and the arrangement of the music. Little did I know then that music was to become a big part of my life.

I slipped out when the song had ended, I must have been completely invisible to the other children.

The next day I was on cleaning duty, my task was to polish the grand staircase with a polishing machine, it had a single headed brush with a very long electric cable. I had never seen one of these machines before in my life, an 8-year-old child given this task is quite unbelievable. I was shown what to do by one of the older girls and was left to it. I pressed the button to on, the machine took on a life of its own bouncing here there and everywhere, my heart was pounding in my chest, I found it hard to control but after many attempts to control it, I finally got the gist. I did find it hard at first but mastered it in the end.

A lot of the children there at the time had many problems and acted in the strangest of ways. I made sure that I did not make it my business to find out why they were there, until one day the most strange event took place that has been scorched into my memory ever since; I remember this as if it happened yesterday rather than 45 years ago.

I was in the drawing room which held a full size snooker table; the boys used this more than the girls. I was sitting at the back near the window looking out onto the courtyard that led onto the most beautiful gardens that had a Victorian layout, when I saw this very tall thin girl who was shuffling rather than walking. She had dark, short cropped black hair and looked so deathly pale, wearing this very crumpled up grey cardigan with her hands crossed over her chest and spit drooling out of her mouth making these strange noises. The minute she entered the drawing room there was a sudden strong stench of shit and piss, it was so bad it was stinging my nose.

Then this chanting by the other children started, "Shitty knickers, shitty knickers, shitty knickers." The girl became very upset so much so that she started screaming out hysterically and throwing herself on the floor and smashing herself against the wall. It was then that I noticed she had shit all over her hands, clothes and the baggy nylon trousers she was wearing, also at the same time, diarrhoea was pouring out from the bottom of her trousers. Within moments, staff came running in taking hold of this poor unfortunate person and led her away quickly and this left me a bit in a traumatized way and feeling very sorry for the girl. An older girl approached me and started speaking to me, yes me, I could not believe it, I had been invisible for weeks yet I became visible that day.

The girl told me that shitty knickers was on heavy medication and slept in the yellow dorm that she was in. The girls that shared the dorm were getting fed up with all the shit and piss smells in the room and that the girl regularly messed the bed, the reception centre were waiting to get her placed in the right centre to cope with her needs. I was also told that the girl had been abused by a lot of men, I of course did not understand what she really meant, she was a lot older than me, but whatever it meant, it was enough for me to decide to just stay away from the girl.

I was settling down into the reception centre even though it was packed with children. I was there but never quite part of it, never made any friends and it certainly was not for want of trying; I was desperate to make friends but this was not going to happen.

Saturdays was the day we received pocket money with our names on, in the little brown packets that were handed over to us. On this day along with the older children we were allowed to go out to the main town centre to spend our pocket money. I just followed the other children and duly spent my pocket money; it was fun but even though I tagged along with the other children, I was still very much on my own.

I remember buying my first record a single by Freda Payne, Band of Gold. I did not have anything to play it on, so I thought to myself that I would ask one of the older girls in the yellow dorm if it could be played on their record player.

After looking around the town centre, I noticed everyone had gathered up outside the record shop. I took that as the signal that it was time to go and head back. We arrived at one of the back alleyways which was a short cut back to the children's home behind the back of people's houses, rather than walking near the main road as that was very busy with traffic all the time. As soon as we arrived at the alleyway all the children started running down it, I decided not to run with them but walk; I was not any part of them, I was on my own so I might as well walk on my own.

I noticed a girl that had stopped running and was walking very slowly and she turned round looking at me, I caught up with her and she said to me, "I'm Jenny, what's your name?"

I was a little hesitant but duly gave my name, "I'm Val," and we started chatting about what we had bought at the shops, just general chit chat. When we arrived back Jenny said that she was going to put all her things in her locker and would see me later.

I went straight to my dorm and sat on my bed re-looking at the record I had bought and I couldn't wait to get it played on the record player, hoping and praying that the older girls from the yellow dorm would allow me a play on their record player.

I jumped up and headed for their dorm, as I was getting nearer I noticed that it was very quiet, normally there would be lots of laughing coming from the dorm and the door was closed. I took a deep breath and knocked on the door, then I heard a voice say, "Who is it, we are busy go away."

I turned the door handle and stuck my head round the door, one of the older girls said come in, and all of the girls were lying on their beds writing. I asked what they were doing as I walked in clutching my record. "We are writing letters home."

I said, "What are you doing that for?"

"It's what we do when we don't go home for the weekend, you should be writing yours as the office collects them today for posting."

I had never written a letter before, I did not know how to. I asked the older girl if I could watch her to see how it was done, she didn't mind showing me, and after I had an idea, I went back to my dorm to write my first letter. It said, Hello Mum, it's Val, how are you? I am fine, Lots of love, Val xxxx. I had to place my letter in an envelope and put the address on it, that was easy as I did know part of the address, and I quickly went back to the yellow dorm with my completed letter in my hand. I then showed it to the older girl who said I needed to put a stamp on it; I did not have any stamps. This girl was kind enough to give me a second class stamp; I remember I was so excited licking the stamp and proudly placing it on the envelope.

The rest of the girls had finished writing their letters and the eldest girl collected them all up mine included and said she wouldn't be long and would hand it into the office for the letters to be posted today.

I sat down on her bed waiting so I could ask her if she would play my record on her record player. As soon as she came back I asked the question and to my surprise she said yes. I flew out of the dorm as fast as my legs would allow me.

I was so happy as my record was duly played, I thanked her and left.

I was getting bored, there was not much to do, and I decided that I would go and sit outside in the courtyard.

It was not long before Jenny came outside and sat on the wall with me, she was also bored and we both kept staring at the wonderful apple tree standing there with its arms outstretched holding an array of lovely looking juicy apples in the colour of red and green. It felt like the tree was smiling down on us saying, come on what you waiting for, come and climb me and get the lovely apples I hold. Climbing the tree was an impossibility as the tree had been cut in a certain way to stop children like us on wanting to climb the tree to obtain the irresistible fruits. My mouth was starting to water and I could not wait to figure out a way to get the apples down.

We both walked round the apple tree eyeing it up and down, there was just no way, even jumping up and down in order to get a little tap to maybe touch one to drop off, we were just too small. I had a quick and sudden thought; if I could find a stone or brick large enough maybe I could knock some apples off that way for Jenny and me.

Suddenly Jenny had found an old half of a brick, perfect I thought. I told Jenny to stand back whilst I threw the brick high up at the tree, and the moment I threw the brick, Jenny ran under the arms of tree with the brick still in mid-air, and the brick came flying down and landed on Jenny's head with a thud. Then screams of pain came crashing out of her vocally, and she was holding her head with her hands and at the point of impact I could see blood gushing from her head.

Before I had even had the chance to get across to Jenny, staff from the reception centre had already flown out of the doors attending to her, with Jenny saying in a distressed state that I had thrown a brick at her head. With that information given in the space of seconds, a member of staff was heading in my direction looking very angrily at me and grabbing me by the arm and telling me to go to my dorm and stay there until the warden came to see me.

I was so upset that Jenny had been hurt which was a complete accident, so I lay my head on my pillow and started crying wondering if she was ok. I was up in the dorm for quite a long time before the warden came to speak to me about the incident. I told the warden exactly what had happened, but he looked at me in a way that demonstrated that he did not believe my version of events and then quickly added that the police had been called; they will be taking a statement from Jenny after she has had her stitches done in the hospital.

Later that evening I was collected and taken to the warden's office and delivered into the hands of the police.

Jenny had made her police statement in which she had claimed that the brick had been thrown at her deliberately with no mention of us trying to get apples out of the tree. I had no understanding why Jenny would have said that when it was so untrue. I told the police exactly what had happened and they wrote it down. I was then told I could go, the warden told me to go back up to my dorm.

I remember going over and over in my mind everything that had happened and could not understand why Jenny had told a completely different story.

The warden came back up to my dorm and said, "You have missed your tea, go down to the kitchen and they will sort something for you to eat, the police will be coming back to speak to you again."

I never saw Jenny again, a week had passed, and I was playing in the courtyard garden when I was approached by a lady and a man; they told me they were detectives and wanted to ask me some more questions about the brick incident.

I did not want to talk to anyone as I was busy playing with my dolls, but the lady detective then said to me, "Why did you throw the brick at Jenny's head, did you want to hurt her?"

I said to the detective, "No I didn't throw a brick at her head, I threw a brick at the apple tree trying to get some apples down, Jenny ran under the tree and the brick landed on her head."

The male detective then said to me, "I believe you threw the brick at Jenny to cause hurt to her, didn't you, it was no accident, it was intentional on your part, do you know you could have killed her, she had to have a lot of stitches."

I said to the detective, "No, I did not throw a brick at Jenny's head; I threw the brick at the apple tree to knock some apples down."

The lady detective then said to me, "There is something very wrong with you isn't there, you like doing things like this don't you, I think you need some special help, we are going to speak with your mum about getting you to see a special person who can help you."

I did not understand what the detective meant with regard to the things she was saying to me, I did not know what could be wrong with me, all I knew was, I tried to knock down apples with a half brick and Jenny went under the tree before the brick came down and hit her on the head.

I remember feeling very confused by what the police had said to me, there is something very wrong with you, they left and I did not think any more about it.

An announcement was made by the staff of the reception centre that in the evening, if we wanted to, we could go on a trip to the cinema to watch the musical movie Oliver Twist. We were all excited and looking forward very much to going. I really did enjoy the movie along with all the songs and the music, little did I know that 14 years into the future I would be meeting and dining with the legend, Lionel Bart, who wrote the script/songs and music score to the hit film Oliver Twist that I was watching at 8 years old.

My time at the reception centre had come to an end and I was told that I would be leaving and going home on the 22/12/1970.

Chapter 6

Come Little Children unto Thee, (Juvenile Court System)

I was back home and in the street, a new comedy sitcom called Love Thy Neighbour had hit our screens a smash hit at the time, but to me it was just a loaded gun giving the public access to pull the trigger over and over again. A new name was given to me, instead of Wogamatter it was the new and "in" names of Sambo and Nig-Nogg along with the signature tune of Love Thy Neighbour.

The endless taunts day in and day out were soul destroying, walking to school and having a bunch of kids singing love thy neighbour and calling me sambo, nig-nogg was starting to have dramatic effects over my self-image; I kept questioning myself over and over again, what was I and who was I? Whoever made up the quote,

'Sticks and stones may break my bones but words will never harm me', was a liar.

Offensive words are more damaging than sticks and stones, as words hurt more and get automatically stored in the file system of our brains that causes permanent damage never ever to be forgotten. Little did I know that the effects of everything I had been through from the age of 3 years old would finally break me down to the full extent of a nervous breakdown aged 17.

31st December 1971, Come unto Thee Little Children. I was due to appear before the Children's Juvenile Court to answer to the 56 alleged offences from 1970 and 1 in 1969 at the tender age of 6 years old. The police supplied the alleged offences, and it was also said that I was the ringleader of the gang, I was 8 years old at the time. Unfortunately, I could not be up before any court and held responsible at the tender age of 8, I could not be held criminally responsible until I attained the age of 10 years old so the 56 offences that the police placed upon me could not be used. For some reason it was all used against me for a court sitting that had been changed to 14th January 1972, so 2 years later the 56 alleged offences came into action.

At the time the law that existed I had to be legally 10 years old; unfortunately for me that law did not apply, so even though I was still only 9 years old, the court proceedings still went ahead with the police wanting my blood, like a pack of hyenas with snapping and snarling teeth just about to rip pounds of flesh away from my tiny 9-year-old body.

I did not have the slightest clue as to what all of this meant, how it would affect me, what were the police trying to achieve at the time.

A solicitor had been instructed to act on behalf of myself and Mum as she was served the summons with my name standing duly alongside.

I remember attending the solicitors' offices and this took all day; it was dark by the time our solicitor was happy with all the information in readiness for the court proceedings. I found it hard going and very boring, going over and over the 56 offences that I did not do- I was not present at half of them, but I would have said anything just to be able to get out of there and go home.

Looking at the 56 offences today, I find it absolutely astounding that some of the offences that the police were kind enough to pin on me occurred whilst I was actually in the Reception Centre (Children's Home). The one that I find totally intriguing was between 1st and 31st August, 1970 namely,

'Removed purse from pocket of coat hanging in changing room at sports field'. How I could have committed this crime is beyond me, I wasn't allowed off the premises at the children's home.

The social worker who was looking after me needed to obtain a school report from the head teacher of the school I was currently attending; the report was needed as soon as possible. The report written from the school was never used and the head teacher was absolutely furious that social services never submitted the report to be read by the judge, this lead to the head teacher contacting social services, the memo reads:-

Mrs. Powell headmistress of the Junior School telephoned social services today at lunchtime and asked to speak to Mr., on an urgent and confidential matter-she would not give details. Mr. did not know the lady, he asked me to contact her for further details. It transpires that she is very concerned over the case of a 10-year-old girl, Valerie Lawson.

On Thursday 13th January a S.W. from the Littlehampton Office (Mrs.) called to see Mrs. Powell, and asked for an urgent report on Valerie as she was appearing before the Magistrates next day.

Despite the short notice, the Headmistress and the teachers prepared a comprehensive report, (one of the most thorough I have done, Mrs. Powell said) and this was duly collected on Friday 14th January.

It has come to Mrs. Powell's notice that this report was not presented to the Magistrates, and she is expressing extreme concern over this; she feels that all concerned are not working together and that, not only was it wrong for her report not to be submitted, but that the best course of action for the girl could not be taken without the Magistrates being aware of all factors. Can you ring her this afternoon please, and discuss?

After reading the report that Mrs. Powell so lovingly constructed 43 years later, I am not surprised that Social Services did not put the report before the Magistrates; it certainly was the most nasty, untrue vindictive report anyone could muster up.

I did not notice any comments of the reporting I had made to her personally about the continued bullying, being beaten up, the constant name calling of nigger, or wog, or being referred to by the teachers as the black girl. She missed that in her report. My memories of this Headmistress were one of pure contempt; she wanted me out of the school.

The constant physical abuse, racial abuse and emotional abuse was dragging me down that much, I mentally shut down totally. There was an incident where I was told to report to the Headmistresses' office, I had done nothing wrong so what did she want to see me about. I waited outside her office until she came out and asked me to come in.

Placing herself seated at her huge desk and upright with a stern look on her face, she grabbed a book opened it and asked me to come round and read this book to her; it was a children's book with large type. It was a book that a 5-year-old child could read, and I could not understand why she would want me to read a baby's book.

I thought to myself in my head, I'm not going to read it, yet I could have read it so easily, I had no problems whatsoever with reading and writing, but I stood there in silence. Mrs. Powell then said in a stern harsh voice, "Read it," still I stood there in silence. Eventually I was told to go and get back to my class.

Never have I forgotten that time spent in her office.

The report Mrs. Powell produced for the Magistrates reads and this is very upsetting to me as it is definitely far away from the truth:-

Regularity of attendance – very erratic.

(If necessary comment on reasons for irregularity and give details of attendance record)

Truancy – a supposition that she is kept home to help.

Occasionally is allowed to stay at home because she does not wish to come to school.

Educational attainment – very poor indeed. She says she does not wish to work.

Ability and special aptitudes – none that we have been able to discover.

Character – Personality and Attitudes.

(a) Personality vicious, calculating and with such a strong personality that she can influence even children from good environments.

(b) Has the child any outstanding characteristics?

She is a facile liar and seems to enjoy inflicting physical and mental suffering on others.

(c) Attitude to teachers and the other children Uncooperative with teachers and spiteful with other children. When her present teacher reprimands another she will get up and hit that child.

(d) Attitude to corporate life of school – negative.

Conduct-

(a) Behaviour in class – disruptive.

(b) Out of class continual complaints from parents of other children about her cruelty and bad influence.

General Health and Physical Standard.

Have you observed any physical condition which you feel affects his progress? If so give details.

Strong and Healthy.

General comments, (Any additional information regarding the child, including interest in sports and other school activities, or the attitude of parents towards the school, which might be useful to the Court, should be included).

Every effort has been made by the school to help this child even taking her to camp mostly at the schools' expense. Her mother has continually been invited to visit and cooperate with the school and has been once only, accompanied by the schools' welfare officer. Promises of her cooperation were never honoured. I feel that this child is beyond the care of a normal day school.

Date 13th January 1972 Mrs., Powell Head Teacher.

I arrived at Court with Mum and my stepfather on the 14th January 1972, what was about to happen I truly did not know.

There were lots of people rushing around, it was a busy place, and Mum told me to go and sit down whilst she spoke with our solicitor and the social services, which did not take long.

For some reason I had a nervous stomach and started to feel very sick, I was feeling fear, but I did not know what I had to fear, an uneasy feeling came washing over me.

Mum tapped my arm, "Come on Val, it's time to go in."

I entered a room which was very big in size, dark with the full lights turned on. I noticed these huge deep dark red fully draped velvet curtains, they were closed and they spilled onto the deep red plush carpets; as you walked on the carpets you could feel your feet sink into them. The rest of the room was in dark deep red oak wall panels, and in the top end of the room were these high benches with a desk, one front desk and two smaller ones at each side encased by panelling enclosing this section off like a big box. I was told by the social worker that this is where the judge will be sitting. In the middle of the court room was a single chair with a deep red cushioning in a lovely soft velvet, it was a queen style chair and was very big. To the right and left were long benches in line with the judge's area, one side for the prosecution and one side for the defence. Behind was an area for members of the public, in my case my family.

I had noticed that the side benches held people placing folders onto their table dressed in dark blue suits and looking official, I then saw my solicitor doing the same with a lot of folders as well.

My Social Worker who was a lady told me that I would be sitting on this chair in the middle of the court room directly facing the judge, singled out on my own looking like a little lamb placed on the sacrificing table awaiting my fate.

That day I was wearing a dress with the penguin dropped crutched woolly tights that I so hated, with a light grey overcoat which I kept on throughout the court proceedings.

I was also informed that I had to stand up when the judge made his entry and to sit back down when the judge told us to. I tried to get onto the chair but found it difficult to get on, but with help from my Social worker I was at long last sitting on the queen style chair with my legs and feet just sticking out; I was not big enough to sit any other way.

The whole room fell silent then shortly afterwards the judge entered the court room everyone rising to their feet and me trying to do the same without falling off this huge chair.

The judge spoke, then the people to the right and left of me spoke, the judge then said, "Please be seated," and I had to do a bit of a backward jump to get myself back onto the chair.

The judge then looked directly at me and started talking to me, I did not know what he was talking about, he then asked me if I understood, I shook my head and said, "I don't know."

I was stuck in the middle of this court room, people were talking in turn from both sides, what they were actually talking about I did not know or even understand, the only thing I knew was it was boring and I just wanted to go home.

All of a sudden the judge said, "Recess and recommence after lunch," and with that, everyone stood up as the judge left the court room.

My social worker came and got me off the chair and said we had to go off to lunch and then come back into court after lunch.

Mum was very upset and angry, I asked her, "What's wrong?"

"Oh Val, you have been blamed for everything by those other kids, I don't know what is going to happen to you, the prosecution is pushing hard to have you put away."

"Why Mum? I haven't done anything wrong," and at this point I started crying, I did not want to leave my family again, my understanding now was that the people in the big red room wanted to take me away from my mum and sisters, and I could not understand why someone would want to do this.

I did not want to go back to the courtroom after lunch, so I said to Mum, "Let's just go home, I don't want to go back in there Mum, please let's just go." I was really crying my eyes out, I was absolutely terrified, the very thought of dorms and wardens made me feel really sick and suddenly I was feeling dizzy, I needed a drink of water.

The afternoon session proceeded with the same rituals as the morning session, I was back in the big chair beginning to feel uncomfortable just sitting there like some stick doll with solid unmovable legs, and becoming more fidgety as time slowly moved on.

How much longer did I have to be in this room I was thinking to myself, my legs were aching, my back was hurting, my stomach was doing continual somersaults, I wanted to go home now. I tried turning round to look at Mum to give her signals, I wanted to go home, but when Mum caught me looking at her she made gestures for me to turn round and face the judge.

At long last it was coming to an end, the judge made his final speech, I could not understand what he was saying, my social worker came up to me and took me off the chair and gave me a hug and took me back to Mum who was looking very pleased, happy with tears in her eyes.

The social worker then said to me, "Val, I will come and see you next week and explain in detail what has happened today in court, I can see that you have been quite bewildered by it all."

"Am I going to be taken away and put into a children's home?"

"No Val, you are not going anywhere, you are going to stay at home with your family, like I said, I will speak to you next week about it, it has been a very long day, everyone is tired, you have nothing to worry about."

As soon as we got back in the car I asked Mum what was going on, and Mum said to me, "It's all over Val, the judge did not believe that you were the ringleader, you were far too young considering the other children are so much older than you. The judge does not believe you are responsible for the 56 alleged crimes, and the prosecution had a right ticking off from the judge for bringing you up before the courts, and you are under the age of criminal responsibility. The judge also said that the other children must be held accountable for their wrongdoings, the prosecution wanted you put away and fought very hard for this to happen with no hard evidence against you, only the statements that the other children had made against you, the judge did put a care order on you and for you to remain at home."

After Mum telling me this I could not understand why they would blame me, they were my friends, the only friends I ever had. I never had any more association with these so called friends of mine again, I was back to

Billy no mates, but I accepted this as I certainly did not want to be in the big red room again.

Much later on, Mum found out that the older children went on to commit more crimes and each and every one of them ended up being removed and placed where naughty children go.

My life picked up where it left off, being beaten up, more racial taunts and once again I was feeling ashamed of myself. Mum married my stepfather and from that marriage along came my brother who I think the world of.

The racial abuse was now being projected at my stepfather that he was a nigger lover, he of course took no notice, but it must have been hard for him as this was happening day in and day out. Mum and my stepfather are still married and have been together for over 40 years.

As far as I am concerned he is simply my dad in every way a dad could be. He wanted to adopt us as his own children but unfortunately this couldn't happen because my natural father made objections, amazing considering he did not care if we were alive or dead.

Mum plunged into a deep depression and was terrified of society and authority; after enduring the court case, the untrue horrific 56 alleged offences, she had given up and kept herself well locked away in the safety of her own home. A transfer had been requested to the council for us to be able to move to Bognor Regis, it was a very long wait.

I had now turned 10 years old and the summer holidays had just started. I was becoming extremely bored, but Dad had bought me a bike, bright orange in colour, I so loved it and would take myself everywhere with it. On this particular day I biked to the marina, there were lots of shops for tourists and restaurants. I looked at this particular restaurant and thought it would be nice if I could work here doing washing up, that would stop me being bored over the summer holidays, I thought about it for a moment and then plucked up the courage to go inside and ask.

"Have you got any jobs going for washing up?"

A lady then said, "Wait here, I will go and get the manager."

I was told to come through into the kitchen where the manager was, as he was busy cooking. "How old are you young lady? We do need someone to wash up for us."

"I am nearly 12."

"You look small for 12," the manager said in broken English, I think he was Italian. "Ok, can you start now, we close at 5pm."

"Yes, I can start now."

It did not occur to me that once again Mum would be worrying about me and if I had started mixing with anyone that was prone to breaking the law.

I loved working in the restaurant, it was fun, the people there were nice, I could eat anything I wanted for my lunch and most of all I felt a sense of belonging, I was accepted as part of the human race.

I did not tell Mum that I was working as I knew straightaway she would not approve of it and would stop me from doing it. Mum did ask where I kept going to out on my bike, but I told Mum that I was just riding around on my own and not mixing with anyone that liked doing naughty things.

Hard times had hit our family, Dad was not working as he was made redundant, Mum was getting very upset as it was getting very hard to keep up with the domestic costs of living and foreign coins had to be put in the electric meter. I felt somehow I had a responsibility to help in any way I could, I had already done my first week washing up and Sunday would be the day I was getting paid.

I did not know what I was paid an hour, I did not have any comprehension of the value of money either. If I was given a couple of pounds for a week's work I would have thought I was rich and that was good pay for all my hard working efforts.

Sunday and 5pm had arrived, it felt like a very long day and I was very anxious to have my money. After everything had been cleaned away with the chairs up on the tables, I was finally given my money in the form of £12.00. I could not wait to get home and hand the money over to Mum so she did not have to put foreign coins in the electric meter.

I was riding high on my bike with a sense of pride, it was a beautiful evening with just a slight cool breeze in the air, and I felt a refreshing feeling come across me with the sun starting to cool down, drenching my skin with the warm gentle air, caressing me all over in the form of happiness.

Mum was in the lounge clutching onto a tissue she had been crying worried about her situation. I had burst into the lounge soaking wet with sweat from riding my bike as fast as I could to get home and give Mum the money.

"Val, where have you been for hours and hours, I hope you have not been mixing with any naughty kids."

I was hesitant to hand over the money and tell Mum that I had been working.

I knew Mum would be very angry at me for lying to her about my whereabouts, the £12.00 had been kept in my hands all screwed up and covered in sweat. "Here Mum this is for you."

Mum looked at what I handed over and seemed very shocked. "Where have you got this from Val?"

"I've been working, Mum, doing washing up. I didn't tell you because I was scared you would stop me from doing it, I'm not hanging around with naughty people Mum, it's only for the summer holidays."

Mum started crying even more, "Oh Val, you are so kind and thoughtful, I could do with this money, it will so help the family out, and this is what I am going to do. I will take the £10.00 and you can have the £2.00, I will have to come to the restaurant to make sure and see the manager myself, I don't know how you have managed to get a job but thank you Val, thank you."

"You can have it all Mum, I don't need it, you have it."

"No no Val, the £2.00 you keep it, you earned it."

The amount of pleasure and happiness that was sweeping over my body was immense and very soul rectifying, it gave me a sense of being worth something with this magnitude of happiness that I was able to help my family in some way and not sit back and just watch the horrific situations Mum had to go through, that felt rewarding. The feelings from all those years ago still stay with me today.

Chapter 7

The Big Move

I was 11 years old and due to start my senior school, much to Mrs. Powell's delight, and of course she had forwarded a glowing report, the same delightful report she had constructed for the Magistrates Court. Mum and Dad had quite a fight on their hands along with the social services to get acceptance from the new Catholic School, they had to go and see the headmaster personally and plead a case in order for the school to accept me.

I accompanied my parents to the meeting with the headmaster of the school, he had a kind face and suffered with severe shaking so his speech was hard to understand. I later found out that he suffered with Parkinson's disease badly. After presenting our case the headmaster accepted me into his school, which meant I had to travel by bus and train to get there.

With the glowing reports from my former school that I did not amount to anything academically, I was placed in the lowest stream you could be in, 1G was top of the shop, 1A next down, 1B and then 1C which was a stream for the less academic students.

On the first day I was due to start my new school, this was the most frightening experience; again I was left to cope on my own, I was told where I had to catch my bus to take me to the train station and I was given a bus pass. Catch a train to school, this was something I had never done before on my own. I did not know which train I had to catch or what train station I needed to get to.

So I arrived at the train station, I must have been early as I did not spot any children wearing the same school uniform as me, and I went and sat down on a green wooden bench inside the train station, and waited and watched to see if I could see anything that would give me any indication as to which train I needed to catch and where I needed to get off. As time was passing by I could feel myself becoming upset and frightened as I just did not know if I had already missed it all or was I just too early.

Children then slowly started piling into the train station going through onto platform 1 wearing the exact uniform I was wearing; it must be there where I need to go I thought to myself. My mouth had gone all dry, my heart was thumping in my chest, but I picked up my school bag and headed for the same platform that the other children were standing on. As I started to go towards the platform a man in a uniform said to me, "Eh ticket or pass please."

I did not have a ticket or a pass, my eyes started to well up with tears, "Ticket or pass, I don't have one of those."

"No ticket or pass, sorry you can't go onto the platform or catch a train."

"Where do I get one from, I don't know, I'm new and just starting my new school."

"Oh right little miss, you need to go to the ticket office to see if your train pass is there, if not you will have to buy a ticket today and sort it out with the school, just round there in the corner, but hurry up your train will be in soon and it does not hang about."

Heart still thumping in my chest I approached the ticket office and explained I was new and was told to collect my train pass here. "Name please, what school?" I gave my name and the school name, "Ah yes here we go, if you lose your pass we will replace it, if you lose it again then you will have to pay to have it replaced, my advice is just don't lose it, there you go, next please."

The train was in and to the left of me. I showed my pass and asked the ticket collector where I had to get off, "Barnham," he said.

I boarded the train and sat down and it was not long before I heard a whistle blow and the train started moving. I kept myself fully focused on my surroundings, what everything looked like from the window, making sure I would recognise everything for my journey home making sure I did not get lost.

The train was moving fast and whizzing past stations and as hard as I tried to see the names of the stations the train had already gone past, making it impossible for me to see what the in-between stations were. How would I be able to see Barnham station if it whizzes past? All of a sudden the train slowed right down and stopped at a station called Ford, I stood up not sure if I should get off here, but the ticket man said Barnham so this is not where I get off. I saw more children in the same uniform getting on, I sat back down and kept my eyes open like a hawk to make sure I did not miss anything and waited until I saw a sign for Barnham.

The train came to a stop and the sign said Barnham, I got off the train as soon as possible, I was so scared that the train might pull off before I had the chance to get off, I did not know as I had never caught a train on my own before. I followed everyone else and eventually I arrived at the school, getting back home I put to the back of my mind for now,

Life at this school started ok, I did not know anyone and really did not make any friends, but I had become accustomed to that and I did not let it bother me either. Being on my own and the feelings of complete loneliness had become a firm friend of mine, it certainly was not through the lack of trying, it was what it was.

Little did I know that I was learning the ropes to pave the way for my younger sisters, I did not want them to go through the absolute sufferings I had to endure.

Being in the C stream was somewhat degrading to me, I found the work and pace of work not challenging at all. I could not feel at any time that my brain academically was being stretched enough and I was very shocked at the amount of students in my class who could not even do the simple things like reading and writing.

As per normal I explored the school grounds to find a hideaway that would keep me safe from potential bullies and the perpetual racist name calling. I thought to myself, I don't think this kind of stuff would be happening in a churchly type of school. Every day we attended church, we had our own church built on the school grounds and my class was taught by nuns and priests.

The teachers had already taken an instant dislike to me as each and every teacher had been briefed by the school report from my previous school, so I never stood any kind of fair chance from this school which does cause a bit of sadness within me, but there was nothing I could do about it.

I proved myself for 2 years and was top of the class, but then everything changed. I was told that I had to sit on my own because it was believed that I had been cheating and one teacher who I will not name said I had been caught changing exam results in his book. I never at any time changed anything, all the passes I achieved were through my own merits from my own academic prowess. After being accused of this I decided to shut down once again, I saw no point of excelling myself any longer.

The 4 o' clock bell rang for home time, I used to cut across the school field to the back entrance of the school grounds, everyone that had to catch trains went that way as well. On this particular day I was walking across then suddenly I received the most immense pain; a lad from my class called Tim had kicked me that hard in the coccyx and ran off laughing, the pain took my breath away. It was nearly one of the most painful experiences I had ever known; why he did this to me I don't know. I was now crying so hard I found it hard to see where I was going. I stayed outside the train station until everyone had caught their trains before I was able to catch the next one, and from this moment forwards I always made sure I caught the second train, that way I would have the assurance of my safety.

I told Mum what had happened and she was very upset and angry that it was going to start up again, me being picked on and suffer severe bullying. "What's his name and do you know where he lives?" I did know his name and where he lived as he was the brother of my sister Hazel's friend, Mum said when Dad gets home we will go round and speak to his parents.

We all went round to this lads' house, Mum and Dad did not know how the parents would react to the reporting of their sons' horrific actions especially where there was no provocation for him to do what he had done to me.

The parents were Italian and were very nice, welcoming us inside their house to listen to what their son had done. In Italian, the father was calling his son to come down immediately, he was very loud vocally. Tim came down and looked very scared to see me in his home with my parents, they asked him if it was true and surprisingly enough he told them that it was true. The father grabbed him by his clothes and said to him in broken English, "Why you do dis tings to dis gal, tell now bambino boy."

"John told me to do it, he hates her, he hates having a nigger in our class, he said he is white power, and if I don't do it he will beat me up and he said I was a wop."

"You tell sorry to dis gal and go, I will sort dis later wit you bambino boy go now."

The parents were very angry and upset that their youngest son had done something so terrible, the whole family was devout Catholics and this went way beyond their catholic beliefs.

Mum and Dad left it with the parents to sort him out; he was in serious trouble as far as his parents were concerned.

A few days later Hazel's friend, his sister told her what happened to him when we left; his father gave him a good hiding with the belt and he was grounded for one whole month.

I did not have any further problems with this lad, thank God is all I can say.

One lunch time I was minding my own business and in the girls' small back playground when suddenly I was jumped on by this girl punching me and pulling my hair and kicking me. There was chanting by the other girls screaming, "Angela, Angela, Angela," egging her on to carry on with her assault on me; there was nothing I could do as it was a surprise attack, I just had to go with it and hope the attack would end soon. When I managed to see who it was, I saw it was a girl from my class, she ran off with her friends laughing as if she had just accomplished something great and mighty. That was it, I had had enough, I decided that at some point I was going to get her and smash her face in.

In class she sat there looking at me sniggering, I looked at her and mouthed "I am going to smash your face in" and after that her face changed dramatically and she looked elsewhere.

At change of lesson she was out the door and gone. I filed into my next lesson still glaring at her, knowing that I was fully intent on paying her back. In fact, I was terrified myself, I really was not a fighter, but if I did not make some kind of stand then I would be deemed an easy target and have a continued life of pure hell at school.

Our last lesson break arrived and I shot off to the library just to stay out of sight of Angela, in fear that she might attack me again even though I had threatened her that she was going to get it from me. I grabbed any book and sat down about to open it then standing right there before me was Angela. I took a quick gulp and was at panic stations, there was no way that I was going to show her that I was in fear, but she spoke to me quickly and said, "I am sorry, please don't smash my face in, John made me do it, he hates you, can we be friends? Look break will be over soon, do you want to come to the toilets on the second floor and have a quick fag? I've got one I pinched it from my brother."

"Ok, let's go."

Things were alright between us and every break we had, it was the second floor toilets until one day a teacher caught us. Who got the full blame and lead by the arm to the head teacher? Yes, it was me as normal, Angela was let off.

Mrs. X, I can't use her name as she is still alive today, gave me a right ticking off, "So you have found your way to me young lady, you will go on report and a letter will be written and sent to your parents." I did not say that Angela provided the fags, I kept silent. The next thing she did was to roll one of my socks down and duly spanked the back of my leg which was stinging and painful, assaulted by the Head Teacher for the girls, there was nothing you could about it except shut up, take it on the chin and go about your business. That kind of punishment was allowed in school life back then, the slipper for the boys or to be hit with a ruler and a slapping for the girls.

I was not safe anywhere not even from the teachers.

The toilets were no longer safe to go and smoke in so the next option was in the fields as far back as possible. Every break we headed to the back of the fields, a lot of other kids were there smoking their heads off and enjoying the moment.

Angela left the school to attend a school nearer to where she lived, and once again my old friend was back – loneliness. What happened next I will never forget. It was quite a cold morning with a deep thick fog and I was so cold; I only had my normal school blazer on, a skirt and long socks. The thick fog was wet and my hair had frizzed up and looked like an abandoned birds' nest; I kept my head down, walking forward to get to my form room. I had a mental vision of sitting on top of the radiators to warm up, it was so cold I could feel it biting into my very bones.

Then came an almighty thud followed by absolutely tremendous pain, I had received the biggest kick right between my legs, a full force kick in the vagina. I felt sick, dizzy everything around me was going black fading in and out and I was just about to faint holding onto my crotch as hard as I could to hold the pain. I heard laughing, it all seemed to be in slow motion and as I lifted my head up slightly to see who the boot belonged to, it was a boy in my class, Peter, who was very tall and standing there with him was John, the boy who hated my guts because I was a nigger. John then said, "I hope that hurt, you ugly black bastard, fuck off back to your own country."

I made it back to my form room still in agonising pain, holding my breath to try and achieve some kind of control for the pain. Every time I removed my hand away from my crotch it felt like something had dropped then a severe throbbing pain would commence, the throbbing in line with the beating of my heart. I'm going home I thought to myself, and I headed out of the form room door and made my way to the train station. It was very quiet on the roads with nobody around. I lost control and howled and cried like never before, saying out loud to God, why God, why is this happening to me, I've done nothing wrong. For the first time I started thinking of death and how much better off I would be if I were dead, at least it would be a better way of being free and at peace.

I arrived home and Mum was shocked to see me back early from school, I did not tell her what had happened, I wanted to spare her the pain and upset. All I said was I really did not feel well and was going to bed and could she please make me a hot water bottle.

The hot water bottle was soothing and I stayed off school for two days until I felt better, but I did have to return back to school something I did not relish.

I was walking up the school steps to get to the third floor and I saw Peter coming down the stairs on his own and I lost it, "You, you nasty shit," and with that I punched him square in the face. His glasses went flying off as he grabbed his face holding the area where I had punched him, "I am going to report you, my glasses are broken, you wait," and he then went running down the stairs as fast as he could, stumbling half way down. By this point I did not give a damn who he told and what he did.

The school held a staff meeting and I was the main topic of that meeting. I was given this information by the Headmaster when I was commissioned to attend his office straightaway; it was 3.45pm and the bell for home time was 3.50. I was more concerned about being late home and I did not like the dark evenings.

The Headmaster then told me that what I had done to Peter was not going to be tolerated or accepted and I would have to pay for his broken glasses. His parents are coming into school tomorrow about this horrific assault, a staff meeting has been held and the school is looking at having you expelled, a letter has been written to your parents.

The Headmaster did not at any time ask me why I had done this, and I certainly did not volunteer any information; I was learning fast that it did not matter what I said, it just fell on deaf ears, something that would happen again in the future when I attained the age of 50 with devastating consequences and catastrophic events held against me by public services.

Mum had received the letter as duly stated to me by the Headmaster, and she was very angry at reading the contents and wanted to know the full facts from me as to why I had punched this boy. I told her what he had done, and I was right, this had a devastating effect on Mum.

She fell on the floor letting out this high pitched scream, crying and saying out loud through distress and upset, "Why can't these white people leave us alone, we don't do anything to anyone, oh my God why? I can't take anymore." For me to see Mum so upset and in pain was distressing and I knew all too well what she had been subjected to and my family, it was heartbreaking to see.

Mum and Dad had an appointment to attend the school to discuss in detail what the schools' intentions were regarding this incident. My parents informed the school what Peter had done to me, and this time the Headmaster said he would question the boy with his parents present and the school would be in contact with them after this had been done.

I never heard any more about it.

I am unsure if the school had anything to do with the next course of events but they were definitely fully aware of it as I found the report written about it 43 years later.

The class that I had been in sent me to Coventry for one whole month. For those who are unfamiliar with this phrase it means this: around 1640 there was a civil war in England, the city of Coventry was Parliamentarian. Royalist (the other side in the war) troops captured in Birmingham were sent for imprisonment in Coventry, where they were ostracised and shunned.

To send someone to Coventry is a British idiom meaning to deliberately ostracise someone. Typically, this is done by not talking to them, avoiding someone's company and generally pretending that they no longer exist.

What I had to endure did not affect me at the time, but later on in my life like a bolt of blue lightening, I crashed in the form of a nervous breakdown when my life was good.

It was upsetting at first as I did nothing to warrant this kind of treatment, but the most shocking thing of all is that the school and all the teachers knew about it and did nothing to correct this kind of behaviour, except one teacher, the only teacher throughout my whole school life who said in his report, "I have no problems with Valerie whatsoever, I find her to be a charming and delightful child, who is helpful in class, causes no problems and enjoys her geography lessons."

To that teacher I am truly thankful – one teacher out of the whole lot, so maybe there is hope after all. Also in the report it is written that the school wanted the whole family out.

The big move finally came, the council offered Mum a 4-bedroom brand new council house in Bognor Regis We were elated to get out and away from the run down council area we had been forced to live in, a new chance, a new start, a new home.

It did not take me long to find a washing up job to do after school and during the school holidays, and not long afterwards all of my sisters were working there giving us something to do, somewhere to go and most of all to be safe from society in general. I worked at this restaurant right up until I left school.

I had a passion for music, I had learnt how to play the guitar, the flute and piano and the dreaded drums and most of all I loved singing. With some of the money I earned from washing up, I would pay to have private piano lessons with a Eugene Carl Portman, and every Sunday afternoon I would walk a few miles out to have my piano lesson, I loved it so much.

After the one month was up at school, my class had decided that they would all start talking to me again; I was recognised, I do exist. By this time, I wasn't really bothered if they spoke to me or not but I refused to be the same as them and duly spoke to them if they spoke to me. I was shocked that John of all people started talking to me, I engaged in conversation with him but I certainly did not trust him.

I am not sure how this came about but John managed to entice me to come to Littlehampton with him and Tim after school. I had no reason whatsoever to go back there considering we had moved to Bognor Regis, maybe I was that desperate to be accepted and to make friends that I fell for it and went there after school with him.

We were getting closer to Falkland Avenue where I had lived before but we were approaching the street at the other end.

My heart started pounding in my chest, I was so scared but I could not let John and Tim see how frightened I was, best to adopt a tough and carefree look.

John was friends with a lad called David who lived three houses into the other end of the street. John knocked on the door and was told to come in, Tim and I followed in behind John. David was sitting in a chair next to the fire, the carpets and the furniture were very old and tatty and very old fashioned, something you would expect to see in a junk shop.

I then realised that David was the brother of the leader of the pack from over the Rec and as quick as I was able to beat my eyes, standing there before me was the leader of the pack, holding a rifle in his hands – an air rifle. I immediately thought to myself, get out of here and run; I was so terrified I must have walked backwards but the door behind me had closed, the air rifle now aimed and pointed at my face. I was catapulted straight back to when I was 3 years old where once again I was standing facing the end of the barrel. The leader of the pack was laughing his head off as he had the air rifle pointing at me. I could not say anything, I could not move, I had frozen to the spot looking straight ahead, he pulled the trigger, and the pellet embedded itself in the wooden door just above my head. I still did not move as I watched him pull the barrel down to insert another pellet and snap it back together all loaded up for the next shot. Tim then said, "Nah I don't want any of this, I'm going home, put it down and leave her alone."

John was standing there with the leader of the pack sniggering and egging him on to get the next shot in, the air rifle aimed at me again. If I did not move this time I was definitely going to receive a pellet in my head, or face or even my eye; I moved out of the way just in time for another pellet to be embedded in the door. In seconds I grabbed the door handle and was out as quick as my body would allow me.

Tim was right behind me, I could hear laughing and them saying, "Did you see how scared the nigger was, shame I missed."

Tim ran straight past me until he was out of sight, and once again I was on my own making my way back to the train station. I was not thinking about anything, I was in a dream like state, numb; my brain had completely switched off and saved me from the trauma of what had just happened, only to reappear later on in my life when I had my nervous breakdown.

I never ever told Mum or anyone else about this incident, I put it to the back of my mind.

At school the next day in the art lesson, John was busy telling the other boys what had happened yesterday with the air rifle. Peter found it absolutely hilarious but Tim just sat there not saying a word.

I sat there looking at John and said to him, "I don't find it funny, but what I do find funny, is that you can't talk clearly with your lisp and big rubber lips, what are you mixed with?"

The whole class heard and burst into an uproar of laughter. John did not find it funny and kept his mouth permanently closed for the rest of the day.

Chapter 8

Life Begins

I had left school just before my 16th birthday, I had taken my CSE exams, I was never given the results and I certainly did not hang around to find out what those results were. Even if I had passed, the school would have probably said I had cheated in some way. 4 years later my exam results came through the post with merits written against each subject. I looked at it screwed it up in my hands and duly placed it in the bin. I had done 4 years without it what possible difference could it make to my life now.

I had put myself into an electronic factory working full time; I liked the work and learnt a lot about electronics, wiring resisters, motherboards, soldering it was interesting work. I had learnt and progressed so well that I was given a very good position wiring up massive Rank Xerox transformers.

I had built my own Hi-fi system from all broken bits and bobs; this was the beginning of my music career. The system I had built myself was to be the most important piece of equipment I ever owned. Each pay day I would be off to the town on a Saturday morning buying myself as many records I could afford, focusing on the artists Barbra Streisand and Diana Ross. Diana Ross was a favorite of mine, Mum would play her records when I was very young; the memory of Diana Ross playing always brought a happiness to Mum which spilled over onto me. Later on in my life I named my son Ross, much to his disapproval as to how his name came about. It is a family joke where he has been saying for years he is going to change his name, he never has.

I would play my records every day and start singing along to Barbra Streisand, to reach her vocal level was very hard as her range was so high, but practice makes perfect; the more I practiced the easier it was becoming. My ears started to change I was listening to music in a completely different way, the arrangement of the music, the strings, how and where each individual instrument was placed, the timing and suddenly I was rearranging pieces in my head, it was magical. My family loved me singing, and the neighbours would listen out whilst I was practicing.

I did not know anything about make up or how to make the most of myself, at the time I was pretty damn ugly, no wonder the opposite sex was never interested in me. I remember when I was at school I was very interested in a lad who joined the school in my last year; I had the hots for him and tried to make it obvious. I made sure that everywhere he was I would be there to get him to notice me, but nothing was working. I told a girl in my class, the biggest mistake I ever made, he was absolutely furious that I could like him in that way, and it was quite clear that he would never be interested in someone so ugly and heinous as me.

I would love to say who he was, but he went on in life to become one of the most famous DJs in England on a top radio show and television.

Since that shattering experience, I started really looking at myself and he was right, I was as ugly as sin itself. I wore glasses that I really did not need any longer, my hair was just a curly bird's nest with no style whatsoever, I still looked like the wild kid from Borneo.

I had a beauty book that I had acquired at some point and decided that it was in my best interests to start learning something from the book; it featured black beauty with pages by Diana Ross. Her words and beliefs to promote black beauty were absolutely life changing for me, all her words to have faith and to be proud of the colour of your skin, how to make the most of yourself, and never be ashamed was having a positive impact on me and at long last I was starting to feel better about myself. I was no longer an alien, I was a human being and I did belong to the human race, and I will be accepted and I will have them falling at my feet.

I started buying the Stage magazine scanning all the pages to make entries into talent competitions, most of them were in London. I would have to ask Mum and Dad if they would help me, I was so excited. I had my hair styled, I had taught myself through the book how to apply make-up and the best colours to suit my skin tones, I was buying the latest fashion, I was looking good for what I was doing at the time.

My sister Hazel was a cross country county runner and knew all the techniques of breathing control whilst running. Hazel, passed away at the age of 46, I miss her so much and it would have been nice to be able to have contacted her for more information and confirmation whilst writing this book. Hazel really did help me a lot as I was trying to establish myself as a singer. I wanted to get my body in good shape and get rid of a few extra pounds of weight I managed to pick up. Hazel then taught me how to jog and implemented the breathing techniques and by using these methods you could run for miles.

Every morning religiously Hazel would run with me until I was strong enough to do it every morning and every evening until I achieved the perfect body.

My first talent competition was arranged, a venue in Walthamstow London. In the car with Mum and Dad I sat at the back with my headphones on going over and over the song I was going to sing in front of the public for the very first time; I was excited and also terrified. When we arrived it was so busy inside, it was a large fun pub that had a tiny stage, piano and microphone, and big massive banners saying in big bold red writing, LIVE TALENT SHOW TONIGHT. I went round to the back, checked in and duly handed the pianist the music score to the song I was going to sing; it was a song from a Barbra Streisand album called Song Bird.

A few girls had come on singing Killing Me Softly and Evergreen by Barbra Streisand, and before long it was my turn. I climbed onto the stage, grabbed the microphone, this was the very first time I had used one and I was not sure how to use it to the best advantage that it offered. The room fell silent and all eyes were focused on me, the piano started playing the beautiful intro to the song, and I began humming to the song and started singing.

I had a big massive applause, whistling and the public shouting out "Beautiful, beautiful." I took my bow, said thank you and left the stage. Mum had tissues in her hands, tears streaming down her face; she was so proud of me and happy. I was receiving proper and positive attention, as a singer and not a nigger, as a singer who had performed the song so beautifully.

All we had to do was watch the remaining acts and wait for the results, did I win or not?

My name was called out, as the winner, and I could not believe it, I had actually won. I was absolutely elated, thank you God, I thought to myself, I know where I'm going now, and I have cracked it, I belong, I belong.

I was still working at the electronics factory and I wanted more from life, God had given me a gift to share and I was going to share it.

There was a lad called Julian who was working at the factory, he was very overweight, I got talking to him and found him to be the most beautiful person inside I had ever met. I looked past his weight problem, he was so kind and caring and we ended up dating each other, the relationship lasted 5 years. He gave me so much love and kindness, he made me feel good about myself and that I was worth loving, I embraced everything he gave me. The only unfortunate thing in our relationship was his mother who actually was a school teacher from my former Junior school. I don't need to write any more on that subject, she did not like the thought of her son seeing me, reminder school report.

The worst thing that could ever have happened to me happened. I was not feeling very well this particular day; I was having a lot of period pains something that I have suffered with all my life. I was sitting in the front lounge with Julian and his mother and then proceeded to have a full blown miscarriage in front of her. I had no idea that I was pregnant. Julian rushed me into the toilet, and what came out was shocking. Julian being the sort of man he was, was so very upset that he had just lost his child. I was just in total shock and am still in shock today about it.

I went to my doctor's and told him what had happened, he gave me an examination and confirmed that I had just had a miscarriage as I was still dilated and this was recorded on my medical records. I told no-one not even Mum, little did I know that this would come up again with my future husband when I was expecting our first child.

I joined a local theatrical group and performed at the Windmill Theatre, I loved every moment of it, but the most amazing thing happened. The first show I did with this group was the Lionel Bart Musical, Oliver Twist. I knew Oliver Twist and all the songs like the back of my hand, I saw the musical film when I was 8 years old. I'm starring in the Theatrical Oliver Twist and I was going to meet the legend Lionel Bart in the future, when he was going to write a song for me, but I did not know that yet. Fate, destiny, I believe in all of that and everything happens for a reason.

A new recording studio opened in our town, Airship Studios, and it was receiving a lot of media coverage at the time. I was still doing a lot of talent competitions, singing at home, keeping my vocals in tune and well stretched and also really going into depth of how to keep my vocals fully protected and how to avoid causing any damage to them as well. If I had inflammation due to singing a lot I would protect my vocals with vocalzone throat pastels, and Triple AAA Anesthetic throat spray which is absolutely brilliant; a lot of artists and speakers use this product, it's like gold.

I was on a mission; I had something I needed to prove.

I was doing three jobs, I would start at the electronics factory at 8am until 5pm, the second job at Chubs factory was 5.15pm until 9pm, I would then rush home, have my tea, have a bath, put on nice clothes, apply make-up, and be out the door at 9.45pm for a 1pm start at the nightclub on the pier until 1am.

These three jobs I held for the period of 6 months, I was rolling in money and had enough to pay Airship Studios for my very first recording.

I had hired all the musicians I needed, and Mum came with me to the recording studio on the day I was due to record a collection of songs, classics by Barbara Streisand my favourite of all The Way We Were, (Memories) is what I call it and I had the worst period ever, so painful and very heavy, but the show must go on. My first recording at the tender age of 16 years old is on You Tube along with a collection of other songs.

It was another scary moment of my life, I had to sing the songs perfectly, stay in time with the music and at the end of it do some editing, maybe re-sing the song or songs if there happened to be anything I was not happy with, or I could do it better.

Once again Mum had tears streaming down her face with pride, "Oh Val, I can't believe it, my daughter a singer with such a beautiful voice, I love it."

From that moment onwards in my musical career, Mum attended every single major recording I ever did and she would always tell me if it was good or bad and go do it again; her opinion was always important to me.

I let my family listen to it, they loved it, Julian loved the song The Way We Were and it is still his favourite 37 years on.

I wanted to get into a singing school, at the time there really was not much about with an excellent track records. As usual I scanned the Stage paper to see if I could find a singing school that had history with a good reputation, and I found one, The Arnold Rose School of Singing in London. I had a few lessons with the Master himself, who was renowned for his specialised singing techniques, breathing control and how to actually open up your lungs, a completely different way to how a normal person would. Arnold told me that I was in the soprano range. At the time I did not know who he really was – just the owner of the singing school. To find out later on in my life that I had been coached by the Grand Master of the world makes me feel so very honoured.

Once again I asked my parents if they would take me for an interview with a chance of being accepted; I had to sing in front of Arnold Rose himself, he saw I had potential and duly accepted me into his school. The private fee was £49 for half an hour's lesson, that was very expensive at the time, but I had three jobs, I could afford the tuition fee.

My life was beginning, I had a purpose, even though I did not have friends really, but I did not let that bother me much at all. Every Saturday I would rise early in the morning to catch a train bound for London on my own, I had to use the underground system, which was alien to me. I was a quick learner and found the right train for Barons Court.

I was working all the hours I could, and religiously attending singing school in London.

On my own alone with my thoughts, I would stare out of the train window, my mind taking me back to everything I had endured, still having no confidence in myself. As far as I was concerned I couldn't really sing, it's an illusion I kept repeating to myself, make-up, nice clothes, latest hair fashions, who are you trying to kid, it still all boils down to being a nigger and a criminal. Nothing will change that fact, all the amount of glossing over will not change a thing, give up, forget about it, kill yourself, oh my God, why were these feelings so strong? I snapped myself out of negative thoughts and placed them to the back of my mind to stay there and leave me alone.

My life was absolutely full to bursting point, I was still doing 3 jobs which amounted to 97hrs per week, I would catch an 8am train on Saturday mornings and return home at 4pm a long day and, somehow manage to fit in gigs for Sunday afternoon at Church farm, plus hold onto my relationship with Julian. I was on the start of burning myself out completely and on the path to a nervous breakdown.

I was tired at work, my main job and I was falling behind and not reaching my target levels. I was letting the factory down and everyone that worked there. If everyone reached their target levels and that was really everyone, the company owners would share with its employees all the surplus bonuses and that could be anything in the region of £100 to £150. The company was a fantastic company to work for, the directors mixed with their employees on a friendly basis, so in essence they got the best out of us and we had the best out of them.

The company director had his own private light aircraft and wanted to share it with his employees, so it was announced that two lucky people could go with him for a free plane ride. A draw was held; my name was pulled out of the hat as the winner, also giving me the opportunity to choose someone else to come with me. I chose a woman called Gill who was most delighted at a chance to go up in the air with the director. That was the first time I had ever been in an aircraft, but what a wonderful thing the director did, he really was a wonderful man and boss.

I had been taken off my job, I was so tired I could not concentrate on what I was doing. A batch of over 100 transformers blew up in the testing bay and as a result of that I was placed on soldering motherboards which I hated because you had to put the smallest resisters in and work at a faster pace.

I started working alongside a girl called Charmaine, who worked very hard making sure she reached her target levels in order to attain the bonus. We got chatting and I told her I was a singer; of course she did not believe a word I was saying. I told her that I attended singing school in London every Saturday, she still did not believe me until I said, "Why don't you come along and maybe we could make a day of it and visit a few places of interest in London."

It was arranged and Charmaine wanted to bring a work friend along, Joan. They both waited outside in the waiting room while I had my singing lesson and when I came out they looked in shock; both Charmaine and Joan said, "Val, you really do have such a beautiful voice, we could hear you singing and going up and down the scales – wow."

We had our day in London and took in Madame Tussauds, I had made some friends at long last.

Charmaine and Joan remained good friends of mine and they never at any time did anything against me or caused me any pain. One day they came out with, "How about a stage name for you," it had never even entered my head about any stage name, but they were right, I needed a name.

Charmaine came out with, "How about Esther St. James?" I did not think much of the name, in fact I hated it and left that well alone or so I thought.

I was feeling strange and could not understand what was happening to me. I was very tired from all the jobs, the school singing lessons, the gigs; I had become bad tempered, snapping at everyone at home and I found that I could not sleep even after the most exhausting day. My mind was noisy, I was reliving my childhood past, it was like watching a movie constantly on rewind, on and on it kept going, sudden loud bangs and I was back to 3 years old, seeing and hearing my father drunk, swearing with his manic laugh as he raised the shot gun, the trigger being pulled over and over again. Just before the explosion, thrown into the mix was the leader of the pack with his air rifle and the loud deafening noise of the shotgun by my father finished at the end of the leader of the packs' air rifle. No I'm thinking in my mind this is not it, that's not how it was.

I would feel a blackness descend upon me, where I would try and see but I could not see as the darkness was zooming in and out from my eyes. I could hear children calling me names mixed in with laughter, teachers screaming at me then it was all slowed down like the tape was playing at the wrong speed. The noise in my head in my mind was so terrifying, my heart banging so loudly in my ears, I just could not stand it, night after night, until I had to have the radio playing all night as this was the only kind of relief I was able to get. It drove my family to despair as I was keeping them awake.

I would get to work looking like death warmed up, I could not physically do my job or any other job and in the end, I had to throw in the towel in. I gave up all the jobs and singing lessons ended as well.

I was crying every day, not on the outside, I was crying on the inside; it was the worst feelings ever. I started food comfort eating and gained a substantial amount of weight. I spoke to Julian and told him a small amount of information, that something was very wrong with me and that I had started taking a sexual interest in females. He was very supportive and reassured me that there was no way I could be gay as I was in a full healthy sexual relationship with him; it must be a phase. Best to go and see the doctor. I said to Julian, "I don't want to be gay, a Lesbian, it sounds like a disease."

I had my appointment with the doctors; I did not tell him anything about my father, the shot gun, the being locked in the shed, the ropes, or the courts. But I did tell him about the noise in my head with no graphic details on how society had treated Mum and me, and also the lesbian interest that I found the most alarming, just the basics, and the crying inside. I was put straight onto anti-depressants with a referral for Cognitive Behavioural Therapy at Chichester Graylingwell Hospital.

The moment I arrived at the Mental Hospital, the appearance of the building was scary, cold looking and even more depressingly, the building was adorned with lots of windows.

The description of the Hospital reads in the archives as this hospital no longer exists and has been knocked down:-

Graylingwell hospital (formerly The West Sussex County Lunatic Asylum) was a psychiatric hospital in Chichester, West Sussex.

The Hospital was built in 1889, and when I attended there it felt like I had been sent back in time to 1889. The first thing that hit me when I entered the building was the strong stench of urine and faeces which I found very offensive, and patients wandering around drugged up, moving slowly in a shuffling fashion, drooling and looking very vacant. Some were in pajamas, some females in nightdresses, and some in white gowns covered in stains.

For a 17-year-old it was so very frightening, I remember thinking to myself, is this how I am going to end up.

There was a very long wide corridor I had to get past, and then a quick turn left that led to another long corridor with more of these vacant frightening patients. One patient had spotted me who had then changed his pathway to the same side I was on, he was looking at me and heading straight towards me mumbling at the same time. My heart was thumping in my chest and I thought he was going to attack me. Quickly I thought to start running, once again I had the feeling of jelly legs but speed took over, I was past him like a shot before he even had a chance to realise I was gone. I saw my turning on the right and shot up the stairs and into the department that dealt with Cognitive Behavioural Therapy.

How I ever managed to get well through therapy is beyond me. I had to endure the scary procedure of getting through the corridors to attend my appointments, then the scary endurance of making my exit back through the corridors; I always had jelly legs.

I stuck with my therapy, but only discussed the bare minimum of information, certainly not saying a word about my father; I talked minimalistically on racial abuse and my father always being in and out of prison and his lack of care and responsibility for his family.

Whilst undergoing therapy, a painful memory appeared out of nowhere. The mind and its storing of information too painful and distressing to be dealt with at the time, to be retrieved when the mind thinks you can deal with it, had re-surfaced.

As a little girl I had started pining for my grandmother, wondering why she had stopped coming to see us. I was missing her so badly and remembering the times that were spent on the beach with her, all the bags of sweets she would bring, I wanted my Nan, I needed my Nan, but she never came.

One day I was playing in the street when this car pulled up beside me unwinding the window; it was Nan with Jack driving. I was so excited, I thought to myself, she's here, she's here and come to stay, I was bubbling with happiness, if the bubbles were visible I would have looked like I had just come out of a bubble machine. saturated with the same wonders that every child would display at seeing and blowing bubbles, it's a kind of magic.

My Nan then said to me, "Val, have you seen your father?"

I said, "No, I will tell Mum you are here, how long you staying Nan?" and with those words Nan wound her window closed and pulled away in the car. I just stood there watching Nan disappear into the distance, receiving the biggest needle to pop every single bubble I had. My thoughts at that time were Nan does not love me anymore, or my sisters or my mum, what did we do wrong. Tears came to my eyes and then I cried like I have never cried before. My therapist told me that was perfectly normal, and that I was crying old tears.

I talked about the lesbian feelings I was having; I did not want to be gay. As we went through some of the basics of what I had endured, it was discovered that I was conditioned into being gay as I saw and received a lot of violence from males, my mind going into protection mode decided I would be safer with females.

The long amount of time I spent in therapy as far as I was concerned did not appear to be working, but I stuck with it as I was desperate to get well and get on with my life.

It really did happen like this; all of a sudden I was feeling much better, I was not gay, I could now get on with my life moving forward and never look back.

I came off the anti-depressants, I was sleeping, and feeling positive, the only residue that the therapy left behind was that I would be constantly analysing everything and placing it in boxes.

I was not working and was not interested in doing any kind of job at the moment, I had just got over a breakdown and really needed time for rest, to re-charge the battery then look for work and get back into music.

Mum was getting depressed and felt very lonely and isolated by society; she was alive and living in the world but never quite in it or part of it, but standing at the side waiting to make some entrance into the world if she could. It was if the world was a spinning rollercoaster and she was waiting for an opportunity to grab a ride, but very afraid to take the chance just in case it ended up as a white knuckle ride. As far as I am concerned, life itself is a rollercoaster, you just have to learn to hold on tight with both hands, griping hard to make sure you don't come flying off. And if you come off you get up and wait for the next ride, making sure you have an understanding of why you came off in the first place.

Not working gave me time with Mum and the circle had returned once more, just Mum and me giving each other support and strength to move on together.

I will never forget the wonderful times we had shared together, it was not mother and daughter, we were like best friends. We would go out in the afternoons, treat ourselves to the cinema matinees coming out at the start of the early evening, taking in lunches, shopping, coffees, living a bit and feeling not threatened in any way, shape or form.

Mum would start to worry that she had not been home and had the family's evening meal prepared and I would tell Mum her life was not only about preparing the family meals and home duties, she has a life as well with the right to live it and do something for herself.

Mum started opening up to me, relaying the things she wanted to do. Mum did not ask for much. When she told me what she wanted to do, I laughed, not in any kind of offensive way: Mum in a humble way only wanted to work, to be part of the work force, just to be part of it and earn her own money, but she was terrified that society would not allow it.

From that moment onwards I decided that I would look for a job for both of us. I found a job at the Butlins Holiday Camp, so I told Mum we had an interview to go to. Mum told me, "Val, I can't go, what if the people don't like me because of my colour, they will not give me a job, I can't go, I am too scared."

"Mum, you will get the job, don't be afraid, I will be with you, come on Mum, if you don't try you will never know."

Mum and I were now official 'Chalet Monsters' at Butlins Holiday Camp, Chalet cleaners, but the job had a nickname, chalet monsters, cleaning out all the chalets for the holidaymakers. Mum had her row of chalets and I had mine, and in between I would always go and have a quick check to see how Mum was getting on. We would meet for our morning coffee breaks, and for our lunches we would go to the main staff cafeteria for our free meals.

Mum was an official worker paying her taxes and national insurance contributions, she was elated that finally she could put back into the state system which had supported her and her children, happy and feeling proud of herself, beaming with confidence and getting stronger and stronger, it was a magical moment to witness.

I am so proud of Mum, she went from strength to strength and acquired the reputation of being one of the fastest and most meticulous cleaners with 100% quality, providing the highest standards and service anyone could attain. The management were so pleased with the standards Mum produced that they moved her onto the more expensive chalets that would usually be a job for two people but Mum was that fast, she did the job on her own.

When I was planning on leaving, my sister took up where I left off, Mum teaching Hazel the ropes of the job. Mum was given the task of training up all the new ones that came in.

By this time I had had enough of being a chalet monster and decided I wanted to move onto bigger and better things. I ended up working at a mushroom farm picking mushrooms. At first I was absolutely mesmerized by it all, going into dark sheds and seeing all these different kinds of mushrooms, learning how they grew them, seeing the diseased ones and how this would be cleared and controlled. Then Mum asked me to get her a job there as she had had enough of being a chalet monster; the work was becoming far too much for her.

I was still singing at home as much as possible, always implementing all the techniques and breathing control I had been taught at singing school.

It was not long before Mum joined me at the mushroom farm. She was nervous at learning a new skill; most people would think what is the skill in picking mushrooms, but there is a skill on how the mushrooms are picked and also they need to be picked with speed. I was quite fast, I was teaching Mum how to cut the mushrooms and all the very important procedures that had to be done before entering every mushroom shed; you had to dip all the tools that you used, your knives, your iron trays in a disinfectant solution, and walk on disinfectant walk on trays to make sure your wellington boots were properly done as well.

The mushroom sheds were warm and very moist, so every time you ended up with your hair all frizzed up and there was no chance of looking glamorous on this particular job; I was back to looking like the wild kid from Borneo.

You earned your money by the weight of mushrooms you picked, the more you picked the more you earned. At first Mum was very slow and I would pass over a few boxes of mushrooms to help her with her quota until she had picked up her speed. I was getting very bored with the job; it really was mind blowing and not mind blowing in the sense of greatness, it was repetitive, and mind unchallenging. I started livening the place up and would constantly have mushroom fights, it was so funny seeing all these mushrooms flying up in the air landing at individuals who were looking up to see where these mushrooms had come from. Whilst I was busy conducting myself in this activity, Mum was getting faster and faster and she ended up being the top picker and the fastest as I was getting slower and slower, with my wages decreasing at the same time.

I was duly sacked, the very first time ever, it was upsetting but who cared, it was a lousy job anyway.

Once again Hazel took up a job at the mushroom farm, she handed back her title of a chalet monster and was working with Mum which pleased me as I was worried about Mum being at the job on her own.

I found a job working at an electronic firm soldering motherboards, it was boring but at least I had a good wage coming in.

I started writing songs at home. I knew what sort of sound I wanted and the arrangements, but these songs stayed in a folder as I was just not confident enough in myself in that regard.

I wanted to do another recording with new songs, originals, in order to open more doors into the music world, so the first thing I did as soon as I hit 18 years of age, was to see a Solicitor to have my name legally changed and to have a proper legal stage name. I no longer wanted to be known as Valerie Lawson/ Valerie Critcher which was my stepfather's surname as this was automatically used as my stepfather was my dad.

Even though at the forefront of my mind I was changing my name to obtain a stage name, deep down I was changing my name to get rid of her, Valerie Lawson/Critcher. I had begun to hate her, I blamed her for everything and had to separate myself from her, to be able to survive and move on from all the past pain I had received and constantly felt. I was suffocating and drowning inside, I had to create a new me free from pain and hang-ups, free from memories.

Mum was very hurt and upset that I had my name changed, but I cushioned the blow by saying that it was necessary in order to carry on with my music and it was a much needed stage name.

Esther St. James had now come into being; it felt great, like a second skin. I was loving the feelings that came along with my new name, I exuded confidence, determination and strength, it was as if this new person had taken over and was showing me the new ropes in life and exactly where I was heading. Full steam ahead she would say, I will show them.

Had this person really taken over Valerie, or was it something that was always there and I was just too afraid to show it.

I developed a business head and started approaching companies in order to have full use of their stable of music, written by unknown writers. I got in with a company called.

Carlin Music in Piccadilly, London and got to know this wonderful man Kipp Trevors, who was head of the stables and also a partner in the company. He gave me full access to the stable of music and I had found two songs that I fell in love with. Carlin Music also gave me full permission to record these songs, the only trouble was I did not have a producer but Kipp was so helpful and said to me, "Look Esther, a good friend of mine Peter Lee is a great musician and producer, I will give you his telephone number, give him a call and say Kipp has sent you."

"Thanks Kipp for all your help, I will give him a ring and get back to you."

I called Peter Lee, who went on to do all the music arrangements in the West End show called Cats at the time.

I made arrangements to meet up with him at his home along with his wife Sue, who was a fabulous singer herself. I told Pete exactly how I wanted these songs to go, what I wanted in them and also that I needed some backing singers and Pete said, "No worries about that Esther, Sue and Kipp can do the backing vocals."

"Kipp, you are kidding me, Kipp doing backing vocals, I did not know he could even sing."

"Oh yes, our Kipp has a great voice."

I left Pete to work on the songs and produce the arrangements. I would be sent a copy of a working tape so I could practice and learn the new arrangements and be perfect for the recording.

This was completely different material than I was used to working with; I only ever did ballads, so I never thought I would be able to enter into the world of Dance music, I mean Dance music you would dance to in nightclubs.

I was so shocked how easy it was when I did my rehearsals at home, how my voice slid and glided to all those lovely notes, still keeping a natural vibrato at the same time. I loved this kind of music; at long last Esther had found her niche.

I had a few meetings with Pete and the lovely Sue, and we went over the final arrangements to make sure I was happy with everything, "Everything is great Pete, I just can't wait to get into the recording studio and get it down, which studio will we be using?"

"It's a studio in Berkshire, 32 track, a great place to record, it's on a farm with a great feeling, you will love it."

"Thanks Pete, how much will it cost for the recording?"

"A thousand pounds Esther."

"Right, ok Pete, get us booked in."

I did not have a thousand pounds, what was I going to do. I thought I would ask Mum and Dad if they could lend me the money, but when I told Mum how much it would cost, she nearly fell on the floor, "Oh Val, that's so expensive, it's a lot of money."

"Oh please Mum, I will pay every single penny back, I promise, and don't call me Val, that's not my name anymore."

"Let me think about it Esther, I need to talk it over with Dad, ok."

Talk about living on my nerves, I was anxious, scared, worried that all these people that had been involved, Pete, Sue, Kipp from Carlin who had all worked on this project, that I was going to lose face and let all these people down myself included. I hoped and prayed that Mum and Dad would come through.

Kipp called me to say that we were booked in at Manorcroft Studio in Berkshire for next weekend, was I ok with that date, "All systems are go here Kipp, see you at the studio."

What have I gone and done I thought to myself, I have agreed to the recording date and I still had not got an answer from Mum and Dad.

That's it, I thought to myself, I have to approach Mum and find out where my fate is going, I could no longer cope with the uncertainty, was I going to get the red light or the green light.

I asked Mum if she was going to loan me the money, and all she said was, "I will let you know in a few days."

"A few days, it's next weekend Mum," I left it at that, and thought to myself, what will be will be.

Mum came through with the money! I was elated, excited and so grateful that Mum had given me the chance to move full steam ahead, bless Mum. I was not aware of the reason it had taken so long for the answer; Mum had gone to the bank to take out a loan and that is why she could not give me answer sooner, she was waiting to see if the bank would lend it to her. I am so grateful and will never forget what Mum did for me, to help me get on with my career in the music world.

This was the recording that would open up the glamorous world of music to me.

I was nervous on the day of the recording, Mum and Dad were both there, and all the musicians started coming in and getting themselves set up, sound checks were made.

Kipp and Sue were rehearsing their lines and getting in sync with harmonies, I had to sing the lead vocal so that all the vocals would gel together and it was beautiful, the feeling of all the vocals complimenting mine felt out of this world, and boy could Kipp sing, we were ready for action.

The experience of this recording session was magnificent, the laughter and the jokes flying around, I had not laughed so much in my life before and I wanted more.

The final polished recording blew me away, the production, the arrangements, the vocals were absolutely fantastic, I loved it and the whole recording was everything I had heard in my head; Peter, Sue and Kipp were great.

It took me a few weeks to come back down to earth and realise that the person in the demo was me, it really was. But business head back on, I had to do something with it, I had to make sure it was heard by the right people, so copies were made and duly sent off.

I was making contact left, right and centre, I got to know a lovely lady called Anni Ivel, who worked with Elaine Paige, and Lionel Bart, Ly Ly, as he was known in the business. Anni gave my recording to him, Lionel loved it and set up a meeting over dinner to discuss writing a song for me.

Anni also set up a meeting with Nicola Martin and Bobbie Gee from Bucks Fizz; they loved my voice and wanted to start writing songs for me. I met them at Nicola's home in Harley Mews, London.

The doors to the music world opened up and I was catapulted into a different world, a new dimension.

I took a big deep breath, and headed forward.